MW01137568

Undefined

A novel

JD GOLD

DENVER, COLORADO

Undefined
All Rights Reserved.
Copyright © 2017 JD Gold
v6.0

This is a work of fiction. The events and characters described herein are
imaginary and are not intended to refer to specific places or living persons.
The opinions expressed in this manuscript are solely the opinions of the author
and do not represent the opinions or thoughts of the publisher. The author has
represented and warranted full ownership and/or legal right to publish all the
materials in this book.

This book may not be reproduced, transmitted, or stored in whole or in part by
any means, including graphic, electronic, or mechanical without the express
written consent of the publisher except in the case of brief quotations embod-
ied in critical articles and reviews.

Outskirts Press, Inc.
http://www.outskirtspress.com

ISBN: 978-1-4787-6324-6

Cover Illustration by Susie Renehan

Outskirts Press and the "OP" logo are trademarks belonging to Outskirts
Press, Inc.

PRINTED IN THE UNITED STATES OF AMERICA

This book is dedicated to Ms. Gavin

Chapter 1

I *can't do this, I can't do this*, my mind kept repeating. It was like I was sure about everything that was going to happen. I am going to be made fun of for my clothes, where I live and just everything else, right? That's just what I knew school was about--appearances, right? There was nothing special in my life. I just did what I did and that was that.

If you count this one, I've been to six boarding schools. All were fine, but none were fun. I guess I am a little rebel, that's why I was sent here in the first place. Wouldn't you agree? Now my thoughts zoomed through my head, bouncing back and forth. To think I could really enjoy this was insane. Just beginning 9th grade isn't everyone's fantasy. There's the beginning of drugs, alcohol and you can finish the rest.

"Come, honey."

It was Monday morning and I was ready to get this goodbye over with and not because I didn't love my mom; it was just annoying that my mom's idea of "helping me" was sending me off. But then again my dad left when I was five, so I guess this was her only hope for me.

"Coming." I left my seat and followed her. My body kept shaking, my hands especially. The advisor led me to a classroom; I was able to peek through the window and see the class. Everyone was in their seats, looking at the teacher. A sudden movement caught my eye. A girl with long brown hair and striking eyes slowly looked my way--her face perfectly symmetrical. I could feel my cheeks reddening, and I turned away from the window.

"It will be alright, just go in," the advisor said, and gave me a pat on the back. I quickly moved away from his hand and slid over to my mom.

"I love you, son. Everything will be okay. You will have a good time—just please behave."

The thought of my mom leaving didn't make me emotional. Although I didn't want to be left alone, especially in a boarding school, I knew I couldn't stay home. I would just have to forget it and let it go. But I couldn't guarantee my mom no trouble.

"It's ok, Mom. We'll talk, I'll be fine." I slid out of my mom's hug and waved goodbye. Before I turned I saw her wipe a tear from her eye, and I felt a twinge of guilt. I kept walking until I came into a classroom with more than twenty eyeballs looking at me. My heart became still then started to pump fast, and I hoped nobody noticed what happened outside. I noticed a quick stare from the girl before I dozed off into a daydream.

"Kody.... Kody, introduce yourself." I just stared at her. The voice came again. "Kody, Kody."

My eyes turned back to the teacher. "Sorry, sir." I said, trying to prevent my voice from straining.

"The name is Mr. King." He stuck out his hand in front of me.

"Welcome to Social Studies class for the next year." He grabbed my hand and shook it. "Go on back to your seat."

I sat down in my chair and looked to the left of me. It was her. I had to know her name so I turned my body. "Hey, I'm Kody, what's your name?"

"Kayla, are you new here?"

"Yeah, my mom thought I needed a break from home so she sent me here. I was failing most of my classes at home." I wasn't telling her the whole truth. My mom recently got a call from my dad who told her he wanted to come back and that's when I found out they were never divorced. I shouldn't know this. If my mom knew she would be furious, probably break down for all I know. She made up an excuse and said this would help me with my grades so that's what I've been telling everyone. I mean it was true so I guess she was right.

"Wow, sounds tough, I'm here because I pulled too many pranks on my teacher." She started laughing and that's when my stomach began to churn. I quickly broke out of it when Mr. King began to talk.

"During class today we will be talking about ISIS." I saw Kayla's mood change because of the way she sank into her chair.

"Are you okay?" I whispered to her.

"Yeah, I love action and everything, but killers and terrorists—not really my thing." Kayla smiled slightly and looked back at the teacher.

"Anybody want to tell me what has been going on with the group ISIS?" Nobody raised their hands. Everybody just seemed to be staring at one another waiting. I unwillingly raised my hand.

"Yes, Mr. Kidd?"

"ISIS is a group of bad people, they kill, they hunt…"

"Yes, we know that. I asked what has been going on."

I rolled my eyes and giggles from the crowd erupted. I wanted to hit Mr. King. From the corner of my eye, I saw Kayla drawing a picture. I focused on it and said. "May I continue?"

"Be my guest," Mr. King said, interested in what I was going to say.

"As we know, they are a bad group, so recently, they have been capturing reporters in their location, locking them up and broadcasting their deaths to the world."

"Yes, Mr. Kidd, well done." I sat back in the chair, interlaced fingers behind my head.

The loud sound of the bell almost knocked me out of my seat. I didn't know where my next class was so I asked a boy beside me--Carter, with blonde hair and brown eyes. He wore a pair of $600 shoes and I know because I've wanted them for the past five years. "Hey, could you help me find my next class?"

"Let me see your schedule." I showed him my schedule and he looked at period 2. "You're with me, Spanish next." I walked beside him, trying to locate Kayla, but I couldn't find her.

"What's wrong with your shoes, man?" Carter said. I looked at Carter's nice shoes once again.

"Dude, shut up," I said.

He didn't say anything after that. We entered the room and he sat down, I picked the closest seat to the door in order to get out as soon as the bell rang. As I sat down, I saw a kid in the seat next to me. I had heard his name before in Mr. King's class: Dustin, brown hair and blue eyes. He always spoke out. Deep down I knew he was like me, the one that called out, the one that didn't care about anything, and the one that no one could count on. It was tough back at home. I didn't really fit in, yet I did get the good ladies. Thinking of Kayla, she was different. I usually dated blondes in my day, but she was better than any blonde I had ever seen or dated.

So as we were in class, I tried talking to him, but all

class period he just sat there, looking down and playing on his phone. Class wasn't so great either, just another lesson about Romeo and Juliet. I've heard the story so many times, I'm just so over it. When the bell finally rang, I walked out of the classroom and followed Dustin. "Hey Dustin, wait up."

"What do you want?"

"Dude, chill." He looked at me.

"You're right, sorry. So what's your problem?"

"My mom sent me here because I was failing all my classes; she thinks this stupid-ass boarding school would help me."

"That's what I'm talkin 'bout. I was sent here because I didn't do my homework and played hooky a few times. It was fun, I smoked and chilled at the skate park." We stopped by his locker and I pretended I hadn't heard that last part.

"Kody, I'm joking."

I laughed.

"Except for the hooky and no school work."

"Looks like were gonna be great friends." I slapped the locker and we continued walking. I couldn't believe I just slapped a locker. I put my hands over my face. We went to the lunchroom and sat at a table together. I saw Kayla walking through the cafeteria with her friend. Dustin lifted up his head and wiped his mouth with his t-shirt.

"Looks like you got a crush alreac

"Not really, she just seems interes

"Why don't you go talk to her?" H and motioned with his hands for me to stayed in my seat.

"Haven't you ever heard of playing

Dustin snorted and we both laugh help but look over one more time to fin back at me. She smiled and I nodded to he our lunches and headed back to class.

Chapter 2

Class was over and so was I. I wanted to go home; this stupid school wasn't getting me anywhere. My stomach started to rumble and the thought of food passed my mind. But it was weird because lunch was an hour ago. However, I went to the cafeteria and met up with Dustin. "Who's your roommate?" he asked.

"Crap, I have no idea." I grabbed an apple and put it in my backpack. Then I ran to the principal's office and got stopped for that because apparently there is a policy of no running in the hallways. I finally got to the principal's office and was called in.

"Are you Mr. Kidd?" she asked properly.

"Yeah, call me Kody."

"Well, Kody, you will be in room eight-C, with Carter." Oh great, this is perfect. I've got to spend a whole year with a guy I don't like.

"Ok thanks." I got up from my seat and opened the door.

"Mr. Kidd."

"Yes?"

"Be careful." A sudden confusion passed my face and I shut the door. I walked to the dorm room 8C and knocked on the door. There was blasting music coming from inside and Carter opened the door. He looked at me with a dull expression.

"I was assigned to be your dorm roommate."

"Alright, then come in," Carter said.

I shut the door behind me and walked over to the empty bed. I placed my bag on top and unpacked. "Don't mess up any of my clothes," Carter said without looking up. Great. This was going to be one hell of a year.

A few weeks passed and my grades were getting better. In my first few classes I got some detentions here and there for having an attitude and speaking out of turn, whatever that meant. All I knew was I was speaking the truth. Probably not wanting to hear it, the teacher's reacted that way. However, although Mr. King gave me a few detentions, his were for different reasons. He was trying to teach me something. My feeling was he wanted to show he was the teacher in the class and had to do what was "right."

Mr. King probably was one of the best teachers I have ever had. When he taught me I got what he was saying, not like the other crappy teachers. I have been getting texts from my mom saying how proud she is of me; It makes me feel good that she knows I'm trying, but I still feel bad she's all alone.

Kayla and I have been seeing each other in the hallways and have been talking a little. Mostly, just questions about homework or a "hi" and "what's up" every so often. But our relationship wasn't going anywhere and that bothered me. I had to do something to show her I wanted to be more than her friend.

After Spanish class with Dustin we walked over to the lunchroom. I walked in line and picked up some spaghetti with meatballs hoping they would be as good as my mother cooked for me. I grabbed a Gatorade and headed toward a table.

Dustin followed behind me and sat down. I looked behind me and saw Kayla sitting down. "Dude you gotta do something, I know you like her."

I wasn't going to deny that. He was my best friend so it didn't matter and he was't making fun of me despite teasing me a little in the beginning of the year. But Dustin was right.

"Go talk to her." He gave me a nod and motioned with his hands for me to go. I took a deep breath and brushed my fingers through my hair. I walked to her table at the right pace hoping my nervousness wouldn't affect the way I'd come off. I cleared my throat and ended up in the back of Kayla. Her friends were talking and then seemed to notice I was there.

"Hey Kayla." She moved her hair out of her face and looked up at me. Looking into my eyes for about 10 seconds her expression changed. Ignoring if something was wrong I asked: "Wanna maybe go out sometime?" I put my foot on the extra room next to her on the seat.

"Sure." Kayla grabbed a pen and wrote her number on my arm. After writing the number down Kayla accidentely spilled her water. I grabbed napkins closest to me and started wiping the table with Kayla. "No, I got it." Her hand overlapped mine. A spark out of nowhere appeared. I heard a little gasp and from the corner of my eyes I could see her looking at me. My eyes forced me to look at my hand. In a second now, nothing was there. Just a damp hand. My mind began asking more questions I couldn't comprehend. I picked my hand up and looked around it. I gave Kayla one last look and then ran, having no idea where I would go.

"Dude, wake up."

I opened my eyes and sat a bit up enough to know who was talking to me. Carter was on his bed reading a magazine with his legs crossed over around his ankles. "What happened?"

"You came running in here and didn't talk to me. You still had class but I covered and said you were sick."

'Thanks." I lay back down on the pillow. What was it? I knew it couldn't be my mind playing with me. I took out my phone to add Kayla's contact because I wanted to call her, but I didn't think she wanted to hear from me. I called her anyway and when she didn't answer, I left her a message. "Hey its Kody... I really need to talk to you,...I know you know something about what happened at lunch." I turned around to see if Carter was listening. "Look... just call me back." I hung up the phone and threw it next to me.

I had watched a movie and sat in bed for almost six hours just trying to relax. Carter opened the door. "Why didn't you want to go to dinner?" He looked on his phone.

I took out my earphones. "I didn't want to." I felt a buzzing sound on my bed and picked up my phone I unlocked it and saw a message.

Party in the "attic"

Address: front house, take straight stairs.

"Are you going to the party?" asked Carter.

"I don't know."

I looked at my alarm clock, 8:00. I grabbed an energy bar to fill my stomach because I hadn't eaten anything all day. I put on a nice pair of pants and shirt; I texted Dustin.

Me: Where are u?

Waiting for a response I unwrapped the bar cover and stuffed half of it in my mouth to chew quickly.

Dustin: Walking out of my room.

I opened my door and left Carter with himself to do what he wanted to do. I looked ahead and saw him start walking, "Hey, wait." I ran toward him and then felt like I was about to throw up.

"Hey dude, you look really bad," Dustin said. I put my hands on my aching stomach and could feel my shirt getting hot.

"I'm fine, a little nervous, which I shouldn't be," I replied, "and I don't feel so well." I opened the door to exit the building.

"What are you so nervous about?" I didn't want to tell him even though he was my friend. I was still afraid that he was going to make fun of me. Maybe I was overreacting, but it was just… just hard to calm down. I was nervous to see Kayla because of what happened. What if what she saw changed her mind, right there, just like that.

"Well, Kayla and I—think I ate something that…" Then something was coming from my stomach. Shoot. There it was. An eruption of vomit.

"Dude, what the hell!" It was all over his shoes and I felt so bad. But I couldn't help it.

"I'm sorry."

"No kidding." He laughed a little. We had to walk way back up to his room but we were only in the lounge area. Dustin was mad because they were a gift from his mom and he'd never had the chance to wear the shoes. So I just ruined it for him. Eventually, we made it outside to the grass without anything happening. "I still don't feel so well," I said, wiping my mouth.

"Not again. " He looked at me and we stopped. "Dude, you're Kody Kidd, you got this. Have fun and be the rebel you are."

I took a deep breath and started walking again. I felt so sick wondering if I'd be able to make it through the party, but I needed to. I *needed* to talk to Kayla. She knew something and I had to know. Dustin and I entered the front house and walked up the stairs. I could hear blasting music and disco lights reflecting off the walls.

"Are you ready for this, man?" Dustin leaned his hand over my shoulder but I moved away.

"Yeah, whatever," I said hesitantly. Dustin walked up the stairs and I stayed behind, looking at my hand. All I saw were my hands with pulsing veins and my light toned color skin, nothing I hadn't seen before. So I followed Dustin and saw a tall black man standing in front of a rope. His hands were behind his back and he had dark shades on with a clipboard on a stool next to him. "Can I help you?" the man asked.

"Yeah, Kody Kidd."

He picked up the list and searched the pages for my name. He opened the rope. "Well, go on in." I followed the red carpet into the room where there was a disco ball, lights and DJ. Whoever organized this party was rich and knew how to do it right. I was pumped up and ready to get wasted--although the thought of getting drunk made me feel even sicker.

I looked for Kayla all over, and even texted her, but there was no response. I told Dustin I had to go find her. I asked around to see if anyone had seen her, but no luck until someone said she was by the bar. I walked over and saw Kayla standing there with a boy; I didn't recognize him.

I felt a sense of jealousy. I wanted to go talk to her, but I didn't know what to say after the incident. I didn't know if she still wanted to go out with me. I turned around to face the shelves topped with different drinks. "Cranberry and Gingerale please." The bartender got the drink and put one of those bendy straws in. I turned around while I drank. I spotted Kayla again still talking to the same boy. Then she glanced at me. It was like she wanted to come talk to me, but didn't. Here it was again. The eruption. I dropped my drink on the floor and ran looking for a bathroom. I knew she was following me. I found the bathroom, closed the door and went to the toilet. I could hear her knocking on the door. "Are you ok?"

I couldn't hear very clearly, but I opened it. "What's wrong?" she asked.

"I think what I ate is making me sick." Maybe it was

the bar I had right before I got ready." She then touched my back and started rubbing it. I began to shake and the feeling that something was coming sent a chill through my spine. I looked at them and there was it again. The spark. Electricity flowing out of my fingertips. "Please stop," I said instantly.

She took her hands off my back. "I knew it." Kayla walked outside and slammed the door. *What just happened?* I said in my mind. Then it came to me. She saw my hands. She saw what happened. But did she?

Suddenly Dustin came in. "Dude, what happened?"

"It's a long story."

"I'll be right back." Dustin disappeared and came back in seconds with a teacher.

"What happened to him?" the teacher said, opening a bottle of water.

"I don't know, I just found him like this." The teacher reached out toward my head. I tried to talk, but the words didn't come; I was too tired.

"Stop, stop," I was trying to say, I kept my hands hidden.

"I think he has a fever." And there it was again, the feeling in my hands. My eyes were becoming blurry and I could barely see him. The next thing I saw was blackness.

Chapter 3

"**G**et him to the nurses' office, now!" I could feel a cold ice pack on my head as I slowly opened my eyes. Dustin was right by my side, telling everyone to back up.

I could feel the flush of hotness overwhelming me. I saw Kayla in the background looking at me with a serious face. She then disappeared into the crowd and I couldn't see her. Then I felt the feeling again; the teacher was lifting me up and it came to my hands. I slid them into my pockets and my head dropped back with no strength to pull forward.

I felt the comfort of my bed. I was dreaming of Kayla by my side rubbing my skin causing the sparks to ignite out of my hands. I suddenly woke up to find Kayla sitting on my bed. Had it been a dream or was it actually reality? "What are you doing here?" I asked.

"I need to talk to you, I saw what happened and I know what's going on."

I was getting nervous, I didn't even know what was happening to me yet, but maybe this was ok. She could help me figure out what was going on.

"Ok, I'm listening."

"Have you been seeing sparks, like come out--of your hands?"

"Yeah."

"My dad had the same thing. I think I also know why you are getting sick. Every time someone touches you, you begin to feel nauseous, but there is a way to control it."

"How?" I asked curiously. Now, thinking about the party, the real torture hadn't started until Kayla touched me on the back.

"I don't know because my father passed away, but I'm sure we can figure it out."

"Did the teacher see anything?"

"I don't think so." It began to feel hopeless, everything did. Was nobody ever going to be able to touch me? Every time someone would, I'd get sick?

"Just go," I said putting a pillow on top off my face to drown out the noise that I heard from being so miserable.

"Fine, I'm just trying to help." Kayla got up from the bed and slammed the door. I felt bad about what I said, but I just didn't know what to do. I lay on my bed until I fell asleep.

Dawn woke me up with the birds chirping and the rooster's crowing annoying me. I sat up from my bed and looked over at Dustin sleeping. I began to feel a sense of disappointment and envy. I wished I were him, without having to worry about anything. I took out my phone and texted Kayla.

Me: Hey, I'm sorry.

Kayla: It's ok, I understand. But I wanna go to the library to do some research.

Me: Yeah, say five o'clock—after class and everything.

Kayla: Sure, just don't talk about what happened to anyone yet without knowing anything.

Me: Duhh.

I was excited to hang with Kayla and find out information. It was like going on a treasure hunt. One had to keep looking and digging until they found the buried treasure, in this case it was answers. I looked at the clock and it was 7:00 a.m.

"Shoot, wake up, Carter, we gotta go." I threw a pillow at his face and he woke up.

"Whoa, what did you do that for?"

"It's seven, we gotta go!" We both got up quickly from our beds. Putting on whatever we could find in the closet. I put a mint in my mouth and skipped brushing my teeth. We got our backpacks and ran out the door. We made it into class in time at 7:30. Mr. King looked especially happy today.

"Class, who's going to try out for track?"

Mostly everyone in the class raised their hand. I wasn't worried because I am a really good runner. I was the fastest in my grade back home.

During class I tried to keep my hands to myself. Like literally. I let no one touch them. I needed to prevent anyone from seeing the spark. Mr. King announced he was going to hand out an assignment. Kayla looked back at me and shook her head. It was like she was saying don't. Don't stick my hand out? Or stick out my hand so Mr. King won't think I'm weird? I couldn't understand what she was saying so when he came over I slowly put my hands out and accepted the sheet. Thankfully, I didn't touch his hands. Kayla had a expression of relief.

I could tell Mr. King was confused about the way I grabbed the paper "Are you ok, Mr. Kidd?"

"Fine, why wouldn't I be?" He nodded slightly and continued handing out the papers. I pulled out my phone in class and texted Dustin.

Me: Meet me outside on the field we gotta get ready for practice.

Dustin: kk

I slipped my phone back into my bag before getting caught by Mr. King.

As soon as the bell rang, I went to my locker to

pick up my track uniform. I went into the gym locker room, changed then ran onto the field to meet Dustin. "Look who's ready to run," I said to Dustin, who sat on a bench outside.

"You know it."

I tightened my shoelace and did my jumping jacks.

"Wanna race?" Dustin asked confidently.

"You think you can beat me? As if!" I said with a fake laugh.

"Any day."

I knew I was faster, but I wanted to let him win. I just thought it would help him with his recent problems. Not long ago he broke up with his girlfriend and I just thought he needed some motivation to think he wasn't a loser. We lined up next to each other.

"We'll race to the orange cone, are you ready?" Dustin said.

"On the count of Three -One, Two, Three." I broke off in lightning mode. I saw Dustin running behind me and I knew I had to ease up. Usually, winning was like a need in my life. It was a thrill that distracted me from my loneliness and kept me from going insane. I slowed my pace and let him pass me right before the cone.

"I told you," he said.

"Good job." He leaned in for a fist pump, but I pretended not to see and flopped down to stretch to avoid his touch.

Then all the guys came out wearing their athletic clothes and sneakers in front of the coach, who was wearing his whistle. I was ready to do this. Running was my passion, I felt free when I ran, not the distance races where one runs in circles, but dashing. "Ok boys, line up, I will be looking at your running skills and seeing who's the fastest and deserves to be on my team. We have sixteen kids and only ten can make it." I started to get a little tense. All the boys lined up to find their space. I followed to pick my own.

"Good luck," I said to Carter.

"Don't need it," Carter said snobbishly. Now it was game time. This was for me. I wasn't going to let Dustin win again or Carter. I knew I needed to prove myself and make it on the team as captain.

"Ready…take your marks… get set…. GO!" I ran so fast, looking behind me. I was absorbing all the air that surrounded me and in that moment I felt so strong, like I could do anything.

There were two guys right beside me and I had to push harder. I lengthened my strides and began to edge ahead. I saw the orange cone and I was first. I saw Dustin right behind me, almost out of breath, panting like a dog. "Did you let me win before?"

I didn't know what to say.

"You know I'm just playing with you, bro, good job out there."

"Thanks, you too," I said trying to sound truthful. Surprisingly, I wasn't even out of breath.

"You, with the purple track shorts, over here now." I ran over to the coach and he tried touching me on the arm, so I faked a sneeze. "Where did you learn how to run like that?"

"I guess it's just a genetic thing," I said proudly.

"Well, good job, kid. You made varsity and you're captain."

Chapter 4

A ll the boys gathered around the coach who announced the players that made the team. "The
following will be on this year's track team: Dustin,
Carter, Benjamin, Taylor, Nile, John, Trevor, Josh,
Connor and, lastly, the team captain, Kody Kidd."

All the boys headed back to the locker room to take
showers. I stepped into my shower and turned the knob.
I loved my showers hot, but at the end I would always
make it really, really cold and then jump out.

The hot water felt so good on my muscles. I thought
I was pretty built up. It was not like I was overweight.
I was just really fit and very strong. My mom used to
say. "Come over here, Red Bull."

Trust me I didn't know what she meant, but it
was pretty funny sometimes. I turned the water on
really, really, really cold as usual. As I felt it pouring
on me, my hands started to shake and the white sparks
appeared at the top of my fingertips. It was so weird.
It was scary for a little, but then I became fascinated. I
tried touching it, and it was so cool and freaky at the
same time. I can't remember the last time I had the
water this cold. "Come on, man, what's taking you so
long?" Dustin asked.

I turned the cold water to hot, and the sparks disappeared. "Just a second," I shouted back. The water went hot to cold again, and the sparks came back. This was amazing. They would shoot out of my hands and just stay there, flashing. I turned off the shower and wrapped my body in a towel. I headed to my locker and put on a nice pair of shorts and a shirt. Although we were meeting at the library, I still considered this a date. Hopefully, Kayla did too. I called Carter and told him I would be at the library and wouldn't be back until 9:00. I walked out of the locker room and headed to meet Kayla. Walking down the hallway I kept practicing what I was going to say to her. "Hey, you look great." No, that wasn't good. "Hey, nice to see you." What was I saying? I looked in my wallet and made sure I had money just in case we went for food.

As I walked into the library I saw Mr. King reading a book. I was going to go over to him, but I saw Kayla come in. She was wearing white jean shorts and this flower top. It was so beautiful on her. Yes, she had makeup on, but she didn't need it. I walked over to her. "You look beautiful."

"Thanks, you look handsome." I tried not to stare, but she was just so gorgeous it was hard not to. "I think I know how we can stop you from getting dizzy when someone touches you." Kayla began to walk and I followed behind her.

Kayla walked over to the fictional-supernatural section. I didn't know why she was looking in that section. I wasn't a vampire or werewolf, but I didn't say anything. She picked out a book and placed it on the table. I sat down on the seat next to her. "So I didn't tell you this before, but when I was taking a shower, I turned it onto cold and the sparks appeared."

"Wow, I didn't know that could happen." She looked confused, but determined to solve my dizziness.

After about an hour I decided to stop because we weren't getting anywhere. "Hey, I think we did enough for one day, wanna go out for ice cream?"

"I think you're right. I'm so in the mood right now."

I picked up the book and placed it back on the shelf. Kayla and I left the library and walked out of the boarding school. As we were walking on the street, I wanted to reach out and grab her hand, but then I remembered the sparks and the sick feeling, and knew I couldn't.

We stopped at the ice cream store and waited in line. "So, how many boyfriends have you had?" I asked trying to break the silence. She looked at me and her face became red and I felt sorry for asking.

"Well, none exactly." Kayla turned back to the line.

"What? How?" I asked.

"I guess I was not good enough for any boy."

"I think you're amazing and any guy is stupid who doesn't like you."

She smiled. We got up to the line and ordered our ice cream. Kayla got a vanilla swirl and I got a plain chocolate soft serve.

I paid for us both and we walked back home. "How do you think this all started?" I asked Kayla curiously. She seemed to take a moment to think about it.

"To be honest, I don't know, my father never told me. He just said why he got sick sometimes, but that's it." I could tell Kayla had never been asked that question before by her facial expression.

"Don't worry about it, let's just enjoy the night." We finished our ice cream and walked back to Kayla's dorm room. "Tonight was really fun," I said as I grabbed her hand; she pulled away.

"What about the sparks and the sick feeling?" she asked. I looked to see if anybody was around. I could handle the pain for a few seconds.

"It doesn't matter." I grabbed Kayla's hands. And there it was again, I felt the dizziness I've felt many times before that. She seemed mesmerized by my fingers and kept trying to touch them.

"What is it?" Kayla asked.

"Nothing, I'll see you tomorrow." I wanted to kiss her, but I didn't. I felt a little lightheaded and couldn't risk fainting on our first date.

"Ok, you too."

I let go of her hands and the spark disappeared. I watched her close the door and start talking to Gabby. I waited by the door and tried to hear if there was any talk about me.

"It was amazing, Gabby. He is probably the most good looking guy I have ever seen, but why me?"

"What do you mean, Kayla, you're funny, gorgeous and you have lips," I heard Gabby say.

"Shut up," Kayla said laughing. I walked out of the girls' dorm and went back to my room.

I opened the door and saw Carter making out with a half-dressed girl. As soon as he saw me he quickly covered his Spiderman boxers with a blanket.

"What the crap is going on in here?"

The girl ran out still topless as I glared at Carter.

"She's just a girl, nobody."

"Aren't you gay?" I asked. I didn't mean to say it, but it just came out.

The girl came back into the room picked up a pillow, and threw it at Carter. "You're gay? You never told me that."

He picked up the pillow and threw it onto the floor and I started laughing at him. She grabbed her shirt and flounced out.

"Why would you say that?" he said, putting on his shirt.

"Well, you're always texting guys and you never talk about girls."

"Well, don't you have your assumptions, and yes, I am gay, but I like to have fun sometimes. I mean, after all, aren't I just handsome as hell?"

That was it. I was about to go out of my mind. This dude was full of it.

"Well, if you want to do this again, can you text …so I don't walk in on you?"

Carter nodded, put in his headphones and laid his head down. I changed into my pajamas and jumped into bed. I pulled out my phone and texted Kayla.

Me: Hey

Kayla: Hey

Me: What's up

Kayla: Nothing much, tonight was really fun.

Me: Yeah I agree. I'm about to watch the Breakfast Club

Kayla: I love that movie!

Me: Maybe we can watch it another time?

Kayla: Yeah, that'd be fun.

I put on my headphones and started the movie. I've always loved the Breakfast Club. I could watch it over and over again and it would never get old.

After watching the movie, Carter came over and offered me water.

"No thanks."

"Are you sure? It tastes like watermelon and candy." After Carter said that I inferred he was drunk.

"I'm sure."

He stood there swaying. "Are you drunk?"

"Maybe, just a little." His eyes were shut and it seemed like he was about to fall. As I got up to go brush my teeth, he crashed into me. The COLD water spilled all over me and the sparks appeared. Shoot. This was not good. "I'm sorry, I didn't mean to spill it." I didn't care about the water right now. I hid my hands from his view. "What's wrong?"

"Nothing." I ran into the bathroom and shut the door behind me. I grabbed a towel and started to wipe my body, trying to get all the water off me. I was so scared that Carter saw the sparks. I opened the bathroom and Carter turned to me.

"Kody, what was that about?"

Chapter 5

"What do you mean?" I asked, trying to sound steady while I took off my shirt and boxers. "Why did you freak out over water?" This meant Carter didn't see anything! This was good then. But how come he didn't? I had to lie.

"Because you got water all over a new shirt my mom bought for me." It sounded better in my head, but I hope he bought it. I threw the wet clothes into the hamper and went to bed.

"Sorry, it was an accident; it won't happen again," Carter said.

I was sound asleep when the alarm woke me up. I didn't want to be late for Mr. King's class and get detention. I was planning on making a date tonight with Kayla, but then I thought that it wouldn't be right if I dated her two days in a row. It would probably seem too desperate. She liked me, but I didn't want to take the chance.

Thank God I made it to class in time. I sat down in my seat and took out my books. I noticed Kayla wasn't in her seat. I raised my hand. "Yes, Mr. Kidd?"

"Where is Kayla?"

"Does that concern you?" I could feel my cheeks turning red after Mr. King said that and I reflexively cracked my knuckles. What was I thinking asking something like that?

"No sir, sorry." I was worried about Kayla. Although I didn't know her very well, we still had feelings for each other and she was part of my life. I mean, saying that was kind of weird. It was a little unexpected, but to be completely honest I did care about her.

By the end of the school day Kayla hadn't answered my texts so I went to her dorm room. She wasn't there so I decided to check the stores near campus. A few minutes later, it started to pour. I zipped up my hoodie and kept my hands in the pockets. I walked inside the ice cream store, looked around, but Kayla was not in sight. My clothes were dripping, but I kept going. I finally saw Kayla on a bench across the street drenched. I ran over to her.

"What are you doing here?" Kayla said when she looked up at me.

"Looking for you, you weren't in class today, what's wrong?" I sat down on the bench right next to her. I wanted to wrap my arm around her, but I didn't think it was the right time.

"Today….like today is the day like my father passed away." I had never heard Kayla not able to express a thought in perfect English. I began to tear-up myself. I knew she needed a friend, so I was going to be there for her. I started to laugh and after I did I realized that it was really rude, so I covered my mouth. "What?" Kayla said.

"It's just, you're really beautiful when you cry." I was being honest, but I hope it didn't sound too cheesy. She smiled and wiped the tears off her face.

"How about we take a walk?" I asked. Kayla got up and I wrapped her hand under mine. I was afraid for a moment, but my skin was covered with my jacket and so was hers so I just enjoyed the moment.

She leaned on my shoulder and calmed down, but was still a little teary.

"I don't want to be a stalker or sound desperate but do you want to go back and watch The Breakfast Club?" Kayla's eyes instantly beamed.

"Yeah, awesome."

I was kind of nervous. I didn't know what the night held for us and I hoped Carter wasn't in the room because that would just ruin everything. We walked into my room and sat on my bed. Carter wasn't there and I got a text from him saying he wouldn't be back until later. This was good. I could have a great evening with Kayla without him making out with a girl again or being annoying all up in our faces. I plopped my computer on my bed and told Kayla to pull up the movie. "How do you like your popcorn?" I asked. Kayla got up from the bed.

"Let me handle this." She walked over to the fridge. " Do you have fruit?

"What?"

But Kayla was already scooping through the fridge seeing what was there. I saw Kayla stick her hands in and come out holding a pack of green grapes, blueberries and strawberries.

"Just wait, this will be the best thing you ever tasted."

I handed her a popped bag of popcorn and a bowl. She poured the bag of popcorn into the bowl and took the fruit and poured it into the bowl. I thought this was the craziest idea ever: Popcorn with fruit?

"Are you sure?" I asked.

"Shut up, Kody, just try it." She laughed. I turned off the lights and sat on the bed with the computer and popcorn between us so we could both watch and eat easily. I stuck my hand in the bowl and picked up a bunch of popcorn and two grapes. I tried it. "Well?" Kayla asked me.

"Shh, I'm watching."

"Admit it; you like it!" She was so happy and gave me a nudge on my shoulder.

"Fine, it is really good."

"Told you." We quieted down and focused back on the movie.

After one part, Kayla started tearing up. "Are you ok?" I asked. I don't think she even knew she was crying because she seemed confused at first.

"Yeah, I'm fine, it gets me all the time." I could tell she was looking for tissues. I didn't have any so my next move was either going to suck or bring her closer to me.

"Here, wipe it on this." I stuck out my arm and she wiped her tears on my sweater.

"Thanks," she said, laughing and stayed in her position. After the movie ended, Kayla got up to go to the bathroom. When she was done, she came out and slipped on the floor. "Ouch."

I ran over to her.

"Are you hurt?" I glanced over her hands and legs and saw Kayla had a bloody scrape on her knee.

"I just slipped, I think the floor is wet." I walked over to get a bandage. I unwrapped the Band-Aid and put my hand on her leg near the cut.

"Don't, remember?" She touched my jacket and our eyes met for a quick second.

"I don't care, you're hurt." I looked back down to see the sparks surrounding her knee. Taking my hands off the knee, the sparks faded away. I went to put the Band- Aid on. "Wait, what happened to your cut?"

"What do you mean?" She looked at me, then at

her knee. Kayla's injury simply vanished. It was like magic, totally out of sight.

"What just happened?" I asked, thinking maybe she would know the answer.

"I..... I don't know, that never happened to my father; at least I don't think it did. You know what this means?"

"No," I said frantically.

"You can heal people!" She jumped up and paced around the room. "Kody-."

"What, no I didn't do that, I couldn't have." I looked at my hands.

"Yeh, you did and you know it."

"How would I know it? Kayla frickin' sparks just came out of my human hands and healed a mark that could have scarred." I couldn't deal. I leaned against the wall and put my head in my hands.

"Kody, it's okay." She moved my hands out of my face and the sick feeling snuck in.

"Stop." I moved to the side of her. "I could be dangerous."

"I don't care, I know you would never hurt me." She looked into my eyes and I had to do it. Her lips were staring at me, calling for attention. I leaned closer and gently touched my lips to hers. It didn't last very long. Our lips separated and I saw a quick flash of the spark.

"I told you you're not dangerous." Kayla smirked.

"I better go," she said. Kayla opened the door. "I'll text you." She gave a smile and left the room.

I walked over to my bed and flopped down. Although the kiss was more than I could have asked for, I still panicked that the sparks were too much to handle, for now.

Chapter 6

After what seemed to be forever, Carter came in, waking me up. "Kody, Kody, Kody wake up there's a fire in the library!" I was so tired, but I pulled myself together.

"Why is there an alarm going off here then?"

" It's spreading, go!"

I ran for the door and tried texting Dustin, but he didn't answer. I hurried to his dorm room and his roommate ran out.

"Where's Dustin?" I yelled.

"Hasn't been in since seven." Then I remembered Dustin mentioned something about a test. I ran to the library, but a teacher stopped me just outside.

"I have to get through; my friend might be in there."

"No, it's unsafe, leave now."

I didn't care what he said or if he was the teacher, I needed to save my best friend. I ran past him and opened the door to the library. The books and shelves were on fire. The smoke stung my eyes and penetrated my lungs."Get out of there!" the teacher yelled. I completely ignored him and kept on running and calling for Dustin as best as I could.

"Dustin, where are you?" He still didn't answer. I

ran into the bathroom and saw somebody passed out. I crouched down and realized it was Dustin. I sat down beside him and tried screaming in his ear. That didn't work. I touched his charred sleeve and shook him, but that didn't work, though he moaned in pain. I looked closer and saw the nasty looking burns that covered Dustin's face and arms. An idea popped into my head, but I resisted it. *I'm not a healer. But what if I can help him.* I tentatively put my hands on his face and the sparks appeared. The burns were going away and his skin was back to normal. Within a few seconds, Dustin woke up.

"What... what happened? What was that?" he sounded scared.

"What do you mean?"

"I... I passed out. How did you wake me up?"

I didn't know what to say, he caught me off guard.

"I splashed water on your face."

Of course he felt his face and didn't feel anything.

He looked at me like I had done something totally wrong, but I drew a blank.

"What do you mean?" I asked.

"I could feel your hands on my face, why?"

"I was trying to wake you up."

He looked confused.

"Whatever, we gotta go!" I got up from the floor and helped Dustin to his feet. As we came across the door in flames, I held my breath and dragged Dustin along with me. I kicked the door open and the firemen came running toward us. They grabbed Dustin and put him on a stretcher.

Kayla came running to me. "Are you ok?" She checked my body for any injuries. "Right here! It's bleeding." I looked down where she was pointing.

"I'm fine, really, it's nothing."

Kayla ignored that."Kody, you can heal yourself."

I seemed to be able to heal people, but myself? Could I really do that? Would I want to? But I couldn't try it here in front of everyone. A fireman walked over and touched my shoulder.

"Kid, come with me now; we need to take you to the hospital." I gave Kayla a scared look.

"I can't." I ran away from him with Kayla following me. I didn't know where I was going to take her in that moment. Where was there to go? Then it came to me the "secret" place where Mr. King took us on the first day of school. "Let's go to the place Mr. King took us."

We both ran across the bridge into the dark woods. Luckily, Kayla had her phone which had a flashlight. She flicked it on and we walked on the road. We made a left and went to the tree where the class had buried a time capsule on the first day of school. Supposedly it was a way to bring the class together.

As we were looking for a place to hide, we could hear voices from far away. It was the police with their flashlights. "Come behind this tree." When I looked around and saw the police we hid hoping they couldn't see us. When I looked around and saw the police officer across the bushes I tried whispering to Kayla, but by accident knocked her over. "Ow."

"I'm sorry," I whispered.

"It wasn't you." She looked under herself. "Kody, do you see that?"

I looked to where she was pointing and saw an oval-shaped box covered in moss.

"Clear," the police officer said.

" We have to look, the boy was injured," another officer said.

"He is not here, let's go." They both become silent and walked away getting farther from me and Kayla.

"Heal yourself now." Kayla broke the silence.

I didn't want to give Kayla or myself a hard time, especially because I had been through so much. I knew I could heal so I didn't know why I was thinking too much about it. Without having any second thoughts, I placed my fingers on the cut; then the sparks appeared.

"Whoa." Kayla looked to my fingers and her eyes became drawn to the flashing light. In a second the cut was healed. It was amazing the way it looked like nothing had been there in the first place.

"Let's get back to the room," I said, wondering why I was whispering.

"Hold on." Kayla turned around and reached down for the box.

"What are you doing? Someone's going to know if you took that."

"Whatever, I want to know what it is." We ran together in the woods trying to find our way back to school. When we entered the parking lot, we walked slowly, looking to see if anybody was there. The fire trucks and police cars were gone so we ran across the lot to the rooms.

Once we were in the hallway, we were going to go our separate ways, but the girls' dorm room was so far away. "Just sleep in my room tonight," I said.

She seemed to be thinking about it, "okay."

I opened the door to my room. Carter was sound asleep on his bed. I went into my drawer and picked out two t-shirts for us.

"Here, use this." I threw her the shirt and she went into the bathroom to put it on.

Kayla came out of the bathroom. "Thanks for the shirt."

" No problem."

"You can sleep in the bed tonight," I told her.

"You're not going to sleep in it with me?"

I didn't know if she was going to ask that question or not, but I was psyched she did.

"I will." We both went into bed and put the covers over ourselves. I made sure to keep my bare skin from touching Kayla. She was chill and didn't look for any sexual attention. However, this wasn't the most comfortable situation. I mean it was totally awesome I was in bed with her, but we only had our first kiss earlier that day. I wasn't expecting anything out of this, but I didn't want to be alone.

It was weird right now because Carter was on his bed, but he was knocked out so that was something I didn't need to worry about.

"Kody?" she asked.

"Yeah?"

"Thanks, for everything."

A small smile crossed my face.

"No problem, anything for you." Then I could tell she had a small smile on her face.

"Could you put your arms over me?"

"Yeah." I turned to my left side and put my arms over her hips on the comforters.

"Kody?" Kayla asked.

"Yeah?"

"Everything will be ok, I promise." Her satisfied sigh gave me a nice sense of sleepiness. I closed my eyes and dozed off.

Chapter 7

C lang-clang-clang. Kayla and I awoke. "What is that?" she asked. I realized it was the stupid alarm clock. I unwrapped my arms from her and hit the alarm clock.

"We gotta go." We both got up and out of bed.

"What am I going to wear? I can't run all the way back to my dorm room." I looked through my stuff to find Kayla something to wear. Maybe she could wear my shirt that said: The Bronx

I handed it to her and she went to the bathroom and changed into it. "How does this look?" She turned to face me.

"It looks fine." I grabbed my backpack and headed off, Kayla was behind me. "Wait, Kody." I stopped and turned around.

"What?"

"The box, we can't let anyone see it." We walked back into my room and hid it under my bed. I met up with Dustin in the hallway walking to first period.

"Hey," I said, waiting to see if he was going to answer me.

"Hey," he said in a flat voice.

"Look, I'm sorry, I can't tell you everything yet, just be happy I saved your life." After I said that, it sounded a little bit harsh.

"Ok," he said. "Thanks."

We walked to class and sat down in our seats. Mr. King came walking over to me, holding up an essay and slammed it on my desk.

"Mr. Kidd, you did unusually terrible on your essay. You have three strikes so that's a detention tonight. You will need to redo this assignment." This wasn't going to be fun, but I couldn't get a call home and let them explain to my mom that I didn't do well.

"Ok," I said.

"Also, I heard you made varsity and you're captain, congrats." It made me a little bit happier when he said that. I was proud of myself.

After history with Dustin, we walked into the cafeteria and sat down. Kayla came over to the table with her friend, Gabby. Kayla sat next to me and Gabby went by Dustin. Kayla took my orange and started playing with it. I wanted to grab her arms and hug her from behind, but I knew what would happen.

"Give me back my orange, or else I won't buy you ice cream." But it was stupid of me to threaten her like that. Somehow she knew I was ticklish and that I would beg for mercy. Then the spark appeared. "Stop, Stop," I begged her.

Then she whispered in my ear. "I'm so sorry. I totally forgot, no one saw. I promise."

"It's ok. I don't blame you for wanting to touch me."

She blushed and ignored my comment. "What about the box, can we clean it tonight?"

I was about to say yes; then I remembered I had detention with Mr. King.

"I can't. I did bad on my paper so I got a detention."

"Well… how about after?"

"Yeah, I'll text you when I'm out." We sat and ate lunch and then went to our Spanish class. I sat down next to Carter and took out my notebooks.

In the middle of class my mom texted me.

Mom: Hey honey, just wanted to check in, haven't heard from you in a while and want to know how you're doing?

Me: Mom! I'll take later, I'm in class!!

I suddenly felt a touch on my back. I turned around and saw it was my teacher who managed to touch my skin enough to make me dizzy.

"Kody, put your phone away." I tucked my hands into my pockets and started to feel dizzy.

"Can….Can I get a drink of water?" I said, about to pass out.

"Quickly." I got up and raced to the water fountain. I drank and looked both ways to see if anyone was watching. The feeling of sickness fizzled down. I walked back into the room and Ms. Ferda looked at me. "Sit down, Kody."

Chapter 8

I walked to my seat and sat down. I turned my phone off to make sure that no one could contact me during class again.

After the bell rang, I started to rush out the door when Ms. Ferda called me to come over to her desk. "Yes?" I said.

"Well, I called you here because I needed to talk to you about your performance, I don't think your doing as well as you could."

"What?" Not again. This couldn't be happening. "I'm sorry, it won't happen anymore, I really gotta go." I ran out of the classroom and opened the door to Mr. King's class.

"You're late," he said with no empathy.

"I'm sorry, a teacher made me stay behind." I went and sat down. I was probably going to be here for a while so I went into my bag and took out my homework.

It was already one hour in. I had finished rewriting the essay and Spanish homework.

"Mr. King, Mr. King please report to the principal's office." He stepped out of his chair.

"Don't move." He gave me a quick stare, then

walked out of the classroom. *I finished the work so what more could he possibly want from me? Screw this; I'm going to see Kayla.* I really needed to leave. Kayla and I were supposed to look at the box.

Kayla: Hey, are you done yet?

Me: Just finished, can I meet you in the room?

Kayla: Not a good idea, passed by a few minutes ago and Carter was with a girl. Not awkward!

Me: Ha ha ha, sorry about that, how about the park?

Kayla: kk, see you in 10.

I placed all my books in my bag and picked up my backpack. I was thinking about leaving a note on his desk, but then I thought that would be a little weird. I knew it wasn't the time to be skipping class or disobeying orders, but what was going on seemed more important. I ran out of the classroom to my dorm room. I tried avoiding all the teachers and when I saw one I hid behind the wall.

I opened the door to the room and there was Carter and the girl. "Sorry, just need to put my bag down." I threw the backpack on the bed and grabbed the box from under my bed.

I closed the door and ran outside to the park. I walked over to the brown bench and saw Kayla on her phone listening to music. Her eyes were closed and she was tapping her feet. I sat on the bench and tapped her.

"Omg, you scared me," Kayla said. She took off her headphones and wrapped them around her phone. Then Kayla grabbed the box from me. "How are we going to get all the dirt off?"

"It's not dirt, it's moss."

"Well, same difference." Kayla said, annoyed. We walked to the girls/boys bathroom and locked the door. I got a cloth and soaped it until Kayla thought it was covered enough to wash it off. "It's working."

"Whoa, what is this?" Kayla asked, running her finger over a strange engraving on the box. All of the sudden, I could tell something clicked for Kayla. "It's... my drawing." She clearly knew that it was her drawing so we both took a closer look at it.

"Look there's a lock, but no key."

I was a little frustrated. We found a box and obviously if it was going to be opened it needed a key. But I had a feeling we were never going to find one.

"How are we going to find the right one?" Kayla asked.

"I don't know, let's go back to the tree where we found it. There might be more information." We walked out of the bathroom. "What are you doing tonight?" I asked.

"Hanging out with the girls."

"Oh, fun." I was a little disappointed. I was going

to ask her if she wanted to go out tonight, but it was ok. Another time.

"Yeah, but I want to hang with you soon." After she said that I was really happy.

I walked Kayla back to her room. "Thanks for doing this."

"Anytime, I mean you're the one that found it." I leaned in and gave her a kiss, but the sparks appeared so I let go. Our kiss lasted about five seconds.

"I'll text you later." She opened the door, gave me a smile then shut it.

Maybe I should ask Dustin to do something tonight. I went to his door and knocked. I heard footsteps and then the door opened. "Hey, what's up?"

"I was wondering if you wanted to do something tonight." The door opened a little more and I saw Gabby, Kayla's best friend. "Oh, I see." I walked away and went back to my room. I fell on my bed and stared at the ceiling. What if I took the box to Mr. King? He might know something about it because he was always talking about old treasure stuff. Although I was sure this wasn't treasure, going to him was the only thing I could think of.

As I walked out of the room with the box, Carter stopped me. "Where are you going?"

"Nowhere." He could tell I was lying. I closed the door behind me and walked out of the dorm room. I tried keeping the box to myself; making sure nobody got a good look to notice what it was. Suddenly I saw the principal walking in my direction.

"Hello Mr. Kidd, what are you doing out on a Friday?"

"Going... to Mr. King."

"Anything I can help with?" She seemed to notice what I was holding.

"It's ok, thank you though." As the conversation ended I sped to Mr. King's classroom; his door was open so I went in. He was at his desk, looking at his papers.

"Hello, Mr. King."

"Hi Kody."

I hope he wasn't mad at me for skipping detention. Maybe he would understand if he knew the truth, but it was too risky.

"So Kayla and I found this box near the secret place you always take us." He stood up as if he knew what I was talking about. He grabbed the box from my hands and put it on his desk, looking at the bottom of it. Why was it so important to see what was on the bottom? Kayla and I had been so focused on the eye that we hadn't even glanced at the bottom.

"It can't be, it can't."

"What can't?" I asked.

Mr. King turned over the box and I thought he saw

something. "It is." I walked over to him and saw the name.

Benjamin Kidd

My father.

Chapter 9

That's my father. Why would his name be under it? I didn't understand.

"Why is my father's name on the box?" I asked.

"I cannot say, it's not the time. You must go."

"What do you mean, not the right time?" He was pushing me out the door. "Wait, I need my box!"

"No, you can't." He put the box in his desk and locked it with a key. In no time at all, I was out of the classroom with the door slammed in my face. *What the heck just happened?* Why would my father's name be on a dusty box that we randomly found in the woods? This didn't make sense and a feeling in my stomach told me it wouldn't. I needed to get the box back. I pulled my phone out and contacted Kayla. I knew she was with her friends, but she was the only person who I could think of that would know what to do.

Me: He took the box! I didn't know he was gonna
Kayla: Who?

Me: Mr. King. He put it in his drawer and locked it with a key

Kayla: We'll find it, I got to go, but text you tomorrow."

Right now there was nothing I could do. I went back to my room and thankfully the girl was gone, but so was Carter. Well, this was great. I was stuck on a Friday with nothing to do, so I decided to call my mom. She was probably wondering how I was.

The phone was ringing. "Hello?"

"Hi Mom. It's Kody."

"Hi!" She was so happy to hear from me, it was like I was at college or something. "How come you didn't respond when I texted you?"

"I was in class and I got in trouble."

"I'm so sorry." I could tell she was sympathetic.

"It's alright, but I gotta go, love you." I was lying, though I didn't need to.

"Ok, love you." She was a little upset and I assumed she knew I was lying. I hung up. Then I remembered I was going to ask her about the box, but I didn't. What was I going to say?

"So I found a box with dad's name on it, anything you're not telling me?" I just couldn't. Now I was bored. I really had nothing to do. Maybe I could catch up on homework. I took out my English assignment and began working on it. We started a new chapter today. I wasn't really paying attention because I had dozed off in class. I took out my textbook and turned to page 548.

The Sign Of Wisdom
-the one with the touch-

I didn't know what the hell this was. The one with the touch? What was that supposed to mean? I kept reading.

Born one day, a small girl about the age of eight wandered out to the brook next to the meadow. She loved to play with the rocks and play hop scotch. A boy then came to her. He kicked down the castle with his foot. The girl became upset. She hit him and pushed him onto the ground. As it started to pour the two ran inside to their houses and the fun ended. Next morning, the girl awoke from her sleep screaming. She'd had a bad dream. Her mom came running in.

"What's wrong, darling?" she asked her daughter.

"I had a bad dream."

Mother stated it was about a boy. The mother sat on her bed and gave her a hug. Her next move was quite unusual. "There was a burst of something--hard to make out," states the mother. The mother walked out of the room and locked her daughter in. The girl didn't know what was going on. She started to cry. The next morning after that, the mother unlocked the door. "Why did you do that?" said the daughter.

"I called the doctor, you need to get checked out."

"What? No! You can't, why would you do this to me!" The girl ran into the bathroom with the mom close behind. She was screaming and putting her hands over her head. She had no idea how all this started. The doctors started to knock on the door. She wasn't opening it. Then they broke down the door.

"NO, NO you can't!" She was continuing to scream.

"The mother's mouth was covered, she was crying," reported one doctor. The doctors took the girl and picked her up. But what about the spark, you may be asking? The doctors were covered in their white coats, so the touch wasn't present at the time. " Doctors told the mother she would be brought back in a week--just some experimenting they needed to do." A week later, she wasn't brought home. It became a month, but she wasn't brought home. "It was the worst choice I ever made," said the mother, "and I never got my daughter back."

I turned the page, but the words didn't make sense. The story never finished. That was weird; it was like the pages were ripped out, but I didn't know why. I closed the book. I was in shock. Was this happening to me? I needed to tell Kayla about this.

Me: Kayla, come here now!

Kayla: I'm with the girls!

Me: It's really important! Please

Kayla: Ok, be at ur dorm in 5 mins

I waited for Kayla to come over, sitting on my bed just doing nothing. It was pretty boring, the sound of the tick-tock going back and forth and the silent white noise that rang in my eardrums.

"Hello, Hello." I heard a knock on the door and opened my eyes. I didn't know I'd fallen asleep, but I must have since I didn't remember anything.

"Come in," I said tiredly. Kayla opened the door and I sat up.

"What was so important that you called me in the middle of my hangout with my friends?" I got up from my bed and took out my textbook from my bag. I turned to the page I marked and pointed to the section.

Kayla's eye wandered over to the page. While she was reading, Kayla was mumbling the words. I was tracking the words with her then looked over to her eyes where I saw confusion, but there was a sign of hurt.

She finished reading and put down the book on my bed. I sat down beside her. "Are you okay?" I wanted to reach my hand out, but I couldn't.

"Yeah, I'm ok. It's just sad a mother would do that. But I don't understand how it all started." I began to think. When did mine start?

I got up, pacing back and forth. "We need to get the box back; there is something inside of it."

"How about tomorrow?" said Kayla. "I will distract

him and ask him about my math homework while you go inside and try to find the key."

"Good idea." I looked outside and it was getting dark. The moon was almost out clearly enough for the light to shine into my room.

"I really should go. My friends might be wondering where I am."

I went to go give her a hug, but it was okay because there was no one around to see what happened. I focused hard on breathing so the feeling of dizziness wouldn't strike me too much. But after we hugged, I was fine.

"Goodnight." I gave her a kiss on the check. Then again, sparks.

I waited for Kayla to close the door to really relax on my own. I put on my PJs and hopped into bed. It was crazy to think how fast this all happened. Every day I just thought that I wanted to go home. How was I going to survive a year at this school until the summer came? But now I had, I think, a girlfriend, and a best friend. Everything was fine. I didn't want to leave anymore.

I shut my eyes and listened to the frog's croaking. I know this was crazy to think, but what if it had cancer or something. *I* could heal it. Just like that. Just with this.

The black room and the dark night closed my eyes shut.

Then I awoke. One thing I had forgotten about: Dustin.

Chapter 10

I didn't know how to tell him. One thing's for sure, although he was my best friend, he still could have a hard time believing me. I tried to forget about the stressful event that was going to occur tomorrow. I just had to close my eyes and fall back asleep.

I woke up and looked to the side of me. Carter was sleeping like a baby. I didn't understand what girls saw in him, even myself in fact. It wasn't like I was Taylor Lautner or Channing Tatum. But I guess Kayla saw something in me and I was really fortunate to have her.

I put on my school outfit and packed my bag. Today was the day when I would either make it out alive or not. That was a little dramatic, but personally it felt like that.

I walked out of my dorm room with Carter to eat breakfast. I wasn't very hungry today. Since the day of the sparks, my appetite had actually changed a lot. I used to be this carnivore that could eat everything in sight, but today, yesterday and the week before there has been no desire for a major meal so I grabbed an apple and water.

Carter picked a table and I followed him. We sat across from each other. I looked up at Carter to start a conversation, but it seemed he was disengaged mentally.

His eyes were peering at a person who must be sitting behind me. "What the hell are you staring at?"

"Wha-?" he mumbled. It was gross, there was drool coming from his mouth. I turned around to see who it was. Of course. Nikita, the girl who was with him in the room when Kayla and I walked in on them. Then his eyes wandered off to Bailey and I recalled the time I walked in when she was shirtless.

"Why are you so obsessed with these girls?" I asked. He lost his focus and then looked straight at me. I guess that comment really upset him.

"Are you joking? How could anyone not like them?"

I turned around one last time. They were not ugly and thinking about it they would probably be the type of people I would go for. But all I could think of was Kayla. It still shocked me that she had never had a boyfriend. It was all really confusing for me. I scanned the lunchroom for Kayla. She was sitting with Gabby and a few of her other friends. I hope she didn't think I was staring, but as soon as our eyes met she gave a little wave. So I waved back.

"What do you see in her?" he asked, disgusted. Usually, if someone asked me that sort of question I wouldn't mind because none of my previous relationships were really meaningful, but with Kayla it was different. Though, hearing the question, I didn't know what I saw in her.

"I don't know. It's a gut feeling like I was drawn to her."

"Ha, knew it. You're just all over her because you're desperate."

I frowned at the sound of that. I wanted to punch him, but it wasn't worth it.

Carter grabbed the water from me and began to drink it. "Hey! Go get your own."

"What if I don't want my own?"

Who was this kid? I know he was my roommate, but seriously he was acting like a five-year-old.

"Just give it back." I tried grabbing the water bottle. He took the cap off and held up the bottle.

"Want some water?" I knew what he was trying to do. But if he did spill it on me then the sparks would appear. He turned over the bottle and there went the water. I jumped off the bench covering my hands with my sweatshirt. I stole a quick glance at Kayla and she could tell what happened.

I looked forward and could hear Carter calling from behind. "Dude, it's just water!" I ran to the bathroom, dried myself off with a towel and went to my next class. I stood at the door waiting for Carter. He came up, holding my backpack with a smirk on his face. "Here's your backpack."

"Don't you ever do something like that again," I said, without even breathing. I was so serious and I meant what I said. I snatched the bag from him and walked into the classroom. I could hear Carter mumbling under his breath. "Dick." I turned and punched him.

The whole class gathered around us. Carter got up from the floor, his nose covered in blood. "Kody!" Kayla shouted. I knew from that, the spark was visible. Everyone could have seen it. Kayla got in the middle and pulled me aside. "The spark, everyone saw it."

Carter came up to me. "What was that for?"

"You know."

"It was a joke, Kody," he said blankly.

I thought he was going to ask me what the sparks were. After Carter walked away, Kayla came up to me. "He didn't see the sparks. But how?"

"I don't know, at least he didn't see it."

Mr. King came walking through the doorway.

"Sit down, class." he plopped his notebooks on his chair. Mr. King turned around to the board and took his chalk marker.

President Of the United States: Barack Obama

"Class, let's start with the basics. Tell me a little about our president," Mr. King asked.

Carter raised his hand. "He's married."

"Good job, Carter."

I couldn't tell if Mr. King was impressed by what Carter said.

Class was all a blur. I was ready to face Dustin in Spanish class. I walked into Ms. Ferda's class, hoping she would ignore what happened last time.

I saw Dustin take his seat across from me. "Hola la clase." that meant the teacher had begun class.

"Hola," the whole class responded. I knew if I got up or tried whispering to Dustin, Ms. Ferda would catch me. I took a sheet of paper out of my notebook and wrote.

Dustin, I need you to talk to me.

I waited for the perfect moment when the teacher was writing on the board to pass the paper. Dustin took it in his hands and opened it up. He took his pencil and wrote something back. He passed the paper.

I just don't understand you. One minute you say you can tell me and the other you ignore me. I just want to know the truth.

How about me and you meet after class outside in the park? But just me and you.

I passed him the paper; he ripped it and looked up at me with a nod. For the rest of class, I focused on Spanish.

When class was over, Ms. Ferda came over to me. "Hello Kody."

"Hello."

She went to the other side of the room into the garbage and took out the ripped pieces of paper.

"Passing notes in class I see, such disrespect." She threw the pieces back into the garbage.

"I can explai-." She cut me off short.

"To the principal's office." I bowed my head in dismay. I didn't know what to expect from this. Last time didn't go so well and I didn't know what she was talking about when she said "Be careful."

"Come in, Mr. Kidd."

I opened the door.

"Please, sit." I took out a piece of gum from my pants.

"Wanna piece?" I stuck the pack of gum out to the principal.

"I'm alright." She folded her hands. "Let's talk about the real reason why you are here." I sank into my chair. Not because I was upset, but already I was bored. "You were passing notes during class."

"So?" I asked.

"Well, that's not acceptable." She gave me a stern look.

"Ok, just saying, I was paying attention in class. It was just very important."

"So important you had to pass notes?"

"Ye-." My phone buzzed.

Dustin: Where are you, man?

"Excuse me. Please put your phone away," the principal said.

"Yeh, one sec." mumbling the words.

Me: Got stuck in the principal's

Dustin: I knew it, just forget it

Me: Stop, just chill, man, give me 2 minutes

Dustin: ok

"I really got to go," I said, putting my phone away.

"Mr. Kidd, I demand you to sit down." I got up and ran out of the room. "Mr. Kidd, come back here!"

I couldn't stop. I opened the door from the house and ran to the park. I saw Dustin sitting on the bench.

"Hey," I said, sitting down.

"So, I have a date, either you tell me what's wrong or I leave now."

"No, listen to me. What I'm about to show you, you can't tell anyone about. Come with me." I walked away from the bench and motioned Dustin to follow me. We walked beside each other. I couldn't tell whether he was confused or just wanted to get this over with.

I decided to go into the cafeteria where there was nobody aside from the people who ate in their free time. I didn't want to be mean about it, but it was the truth. I wasn't going to say fat, but they needed to cut down. All I ate was toast, an energy bar and steak. That's basically my food plan. After deciding it was problematic being in a room with people, I wanted to be safe and headed for the janitor's closet.

"Man, you're creeping me out."

"Just wait."

"Don't you want to turn on the light?" he asked.

"Nope." There was enough light to see where he was and I hoped he could see me. "Can you see me?"

"Barely."

"Good enough. Just stay still and don't move." I put my hands out and onto his shoulders. The beam of electricity almost caused me to go blind.

"Are you gonna show me?" My hands still lay on him, with the sparks blasting.

"What do you mean? I'm showing you."

"All I feel are your hands on my shoulders. Which, by the way, could you take them off?" he said annoyed.

I didn't understand what happened. Had he not seen it? I remembered it was just like Carter. When I punched him no one in the class saw but Kayla.

"Didn't you see that?" I asked.

"See what?!" he sounded annoyed.

"I really got to go."

I rushed out of the janitor's closet, with a dizzy feeling rising in my body.

Chapter 11

I didn't know where to go. I was just so confused. My life was like a puzzle and I didn't even know what the final picture was. I ran all the way back to my dorm room. Almost out of breath, I opened the door and saw Carter sleeping with a bottle of alcohol. "This is so messed up." I muttered under my breath.

I planned to sleep through the night and wake up the next morning with a serious attitude, ready to get the box back and figure out everything that was going on with me.

Clang- clang- clang. The alarm clock woke me up again. It was Saturday morning around 10 o'clock. I jumped out of bed, put on whatever I could find and rushed to Kayla's room.

I knocked on the door. "Who is it?" I heard moaning from behind the door. I couldn't tell if it was Kayla. The door opened and it was Gabby. Her hair was all messed up and she looked exhausted.

"Hey, sorry about waking you up, but I need Kayla." Gabby opened the door a bit wider and pointed to

Kayla sleeping. She was knocked out. I felt bad waking her up. But what needed to get done, needed to get done.

I walked into the room toward Kayla's bed. I sat by her side and stuck out my hand, waving it into her face. "What are you doing?" asked Gabby.

"I need to wake her."

"Lemme do it." She walked toward the bed and sat in front of me. I got up and she started to shake Kayla.

"Wa, Wa... who is it?" She darted up.

"There ya go, now be quiet. I wanna go back to bed." Gabby said with a raw tone.

"Kayla, come on. We have to get the box back." Kayla took the covers off her face and moaned sadly.

"It's ten-thirty am in the morning."

"I know, I know, but come on." Kayla was a late bird; on the weekends she slept until twelve--maybe even later if she could. Gabby was like that too. Thankfully, Kayla eventually got out of bed and within a few minutes she was dressed and ready to go. While walking outside of her dorm house we talked about a plan to get the box back.

"It's gonna be hard to get it back. My math assignment got cancelled because he was at a meeting, but I'm going to need to distract him while you get the box. I don't think the two of us will be enough." I knew what she was thinking, bring Dustin in, but he didn't trust me and I'm sure I was the last person he wanted to see. "We need Dustin."

"He doesn't trust me. I tried to show him my powers and he couldn't see them," I said. She looked confused.

"It's been happening with everyone. First, punching Carter and now this. Maybe they just don't see." It was really amazing how smart Kayla was. But it was a different smart. She didn't do well on papers even if she tried studying, but in odd cases like this, Kayla often found the solution. While we were walking, Kayla began running in the opposite direction. I yelled, "where are you going?"

She went the other direction and through the boys dorm room. Kayla went to Dustin's room and knocked on his door.

I ran over to her. "Stop, I don't want this, Kayla. We can do it without hi-."

The door opened. "Hmmm, Dustin, my man."

"Look who it is." He tried closing the door, only to find Kayla's hand pushing it open. We walked into the room and for a second it was awkward, but, knowing Kayla, she always found a way to make things better.

"I'm going to let you two talk and sadly I'm not going to let you leave until you both make up, whether you're coming or not."

"Coming where?" Dustin forced out suspiciously.

"I was going to get to that."

I gave Kayla the eye, but she was already out the door.

"So, things aren't the best between us right now. But when I tried showing you my powers in the janitor's room, you didn't believe me. First, I don't know why you couldn't see them. Second, I need your help getting something back that Kayla found and is now hidden.

"How do I know you're telling me the truth?"

"Because I see it." Kayla opened the door and hid her face. She looked as if I didn't want her to say that, but honestly I think Dustin would trust Kayla more than me right now.

"Ok, so lemme see this wonderful power you're all talking about."

Kayla walked over to me. I looked at Dustin.

"Come over here." He walked closer to us. Kayla's and my eyes met.

"Are you ready?" she asked.

"Yes." She grabbed my hands and then it happened. The flash, with the sparks. I began to feel nauseous. "Kayla, I can't anymore, stop.... Stop," I said, pain coursing through my body.

Kayla let go and I fell back on the bed. "Did you see it?" she asked Dustin.

It looked like Dustin was about to laugh. "All I

could see was your face turning green and you and Kayla holding hands. What a wonderful superpower you got there." He waved his hands.

I looked back at Kayla in disbelief. I didn't understand. She stepped forward to him and pointed to his chest. "You listen to me, Dustin. My boyfriend needs help and you're going to help us whether you like it or not."

My cheeks turned red. After Kayla said that she looked at me, with redness on her cheeks too.

"Oh, so you guys are boyfriend and girlfriend now," he said, trying to make Kayla feel bad. I did what any "boyfriend" would do.

I got up from the bed. "As a matter of fact, we are."

"Alright then, what about this box you're talking about?" he asked, forgetting his prior comment.

"Mr. King took it from us, w-."

"Your English teacher?" he asked.

"Yes, now we gotta go before he goes into the classroom. You're either with us or not," I said sorta growling at him. Dustin grabbed his coat.

"I'm in." All of us rushed to the classroom to find the door locked. "I'll go into the office and find the key. You both distract the others." By the time we could answer he was running down the hallway to the office.

I looked back to Kayla. "We got this, we need this."

"I will go distract the office people."

"How?" I asked,

"On my free time, I've been helping out with the papers and documents, kinda like an internship," she responded.

"Oh, nice. Sucks you don't get money though."

She chuckled.

"Call me when Dustin comes back."

I planned to stay here until Dustin got the key and brought it back.

Seconds, then minutes passed. I tried calling Kayla—no response and same thing for Dustin. I checked my phone for the time. It was 11:00 a.m., almost time for Mr. King to come and teach weekend school for the extra kids that needed help.

"Kody, wake up." I could feel Dustin whispering in my ear. I woke up and saw him holding the key. I guess I'd dozed off. "Its 11:30—we gotta go," he said.

"Where's Kayla?" I asked, wanting to know the truth.

"She got stuck behind, but she's coming." Dustin took the key and opened the door. We searched all over for the box until Dustin couldn't open a drawer. I tried thinking of other places the key could be. I scanned the room and found a jacket hanging on the hook.

"Look over there," I said. Dustin looked to where I was looking and went over to the hook. He reached in the jacket and found the key.

"Cha-ching," Dustin said, spinning the key on his finger. I took the key and opened the drawer. There it was. The box. "Get it and let's get out of here." I grabbed the box and we ran out of the classroom.

On the way running back to the dorm room, I remembered something. I left the key. We were so close and I blew it. I couldn't go back, but I didn't mention it to Dustin and decided to keep on running. Dustin went back to his room and told me I would see him later.

I opened the door and saw Kayla sitting on my bed. She abruptly got up from the bed. "Are you okay? Did you get the box?"

"Yes, we did." I took the box from behind my back and showed her.

"Wow," Kayla said in amazement.

Chapter 12

"Kody, I don't feel so well." Kayla looked at the floor and seemed to lose her balance.

"Kayla!" I yelled.

"What…?" I looked at her face, which was red as a tomato instead of the usual color white. She managed to walk herself to the bed without me helping her. I heard a knock on the door. "Open up." It was Dustin, pounding at the door.

"Go away," I shouted back at Dustin, but he still kept pounding. Kayla touched me on the arm and I calmed down from the pressure, but felt a little dizzy.

"I'm sorry, but you need to let him in." Kayla let go and I felt refreshed. I laid her on the bed and opened the door for Dustin. He came in and saw Kayla, with her eyes closed, red face and arms dropping to the sides. Dustin rushed to her and sat on the bed. Kayla is *my* girlfriend and he's like all lovey dovey with her.

"Dude, get off of her." Dustin ignored the command and felt her head.

"She's burning up." I walked over to Kayla and saw she was passed out. "What do we do? No one is here, we have to do something," Dustin said. I knew he cared about her and now wasn't the time to worry about it. I had to do the only thing I could think of. And that was going to Mr. King. I know we had just gone in there and he might be teaching a group, but we couldn't go to the nurse because she would ask what happened and we weren't risking anything. "Let's go to Mr. King. I know it's crazy, but I trust him." Dustin seemed to look at me like I was crazy, but gave one more look at Kayla and picked her up.

"Also have something to tell him," I muttered under my breath.

I opened the door and we ran through the hallway. Everyone in our way was trying to get a closer look at Kayla. Dustin was pretty good through the whole thing. I mean I didn't understand how they were so close, but he was definitely being the best friend I had always wanted.

When we got to the door, Mr. King was in front of the classroom. He glanced over at the door and said something to his class that I couldn't hear. Mr. King motioned me to back up. I told Dustin to go behind the door so none of the kids could see him.

Then a group of kids rushed in a pack out the door. They were yelling and throwing their papers behind them. When all of them went outside I walked into the classroom with Dustin following me.

"What are you doing here?" he stammered. I looked from his face and moved to the side. Mr. King's eyes followed to Kayla, passed out on Dustin shoulders. "Bring her in here. Put her on the desk."

I moved away so that Dustin could get through, hoping that Mr. King knew what to do. "What happened?" Mr. King said while getting his gloves, water and a scalpel.

"She just passed out. I don't know what happened, and why are you carrying a scalpel?" I asked. Mr. King put down the materials on the table next to Kayla and opened her shirt. He put his head to her chest and listened to her heart.

"She's still breathing, but barely. I've got to help her and put a tube into her neck so she can breathe." Mr. King slipped on his gloves and opened the scalpel. "Kody, put your hands over her upper chest."

"I can't." Mr. King flashed a look of concern.

"Then Dustin, you do it." Dustin followed his instructions. I was covering my eyes, sitting in the corner, wishing to prevent any cutting or pain. But I knew there was nothing to stop this and that it was the only solution.

Mr. King thrust the scalpel into her body and that was the sign that everything was going to be okay. Kayla started breathing.

After sitting in the classroom for about two hours, with Kayla out on the table with a wet towel on her head, Dustin sleeping against the wall and Mr. King reading the textbook, I seemed to be doing nothing. I got up from the desk and went over to Mr. King.

"What's going on? First, you decide to help Kayla. Second, you took the box from me and now, you're reading our English assignment."

He looked at me like I was in trouble. Mr. King turned over the book and cupped his hands. "There's something you need to know." It was like he had guilt in his eyes and was trying to hold back a secret.

"What is it?" I tried to sound commanding, but could only muster a slow soft voice.

"Not here. Come with me." Mr. King got up from his chair and made his way to the door. He looked at Kayla once more and headed out. I followed right behind him.

Mr. King looked both ways to see if it was clear. Once it was he started to whisper.

"I can't hear you," I said. He then raised his voice.

"I know you took back the box."

I gulped in nervousness.

"But I know why too. There is something you should know. I can't tell you everything, though."

I continued looking at him blankly.

"Kayla's father, I knew him. He had the same proble- or power as you. I helped him contain it, made it easier for him to be able to touch people without getting sick."

I was too shocked about what I was hearing to even move. I even kept my eyes still.

"Then he got caught in a dilemma. Someone discovered his powers. I don't know who, and I tried helping, but it just couldn't happen. A few weeks later, without me knowing anything, he died. People say it was suicide, but I beg to differ. I want to help you."

"How did you even know I had this?" I asked.

The day I met you, I saw a spark in your eye, the same as Kayla's father. I also followed you and Kayla to the woods after the fire."

"Well, how are you going to help me?"

"You will see."

"Does Kayla know about what you think happened to her father?"I asked.

"No, and you may not tell her," he said. "It's not the right time. Meet in the woods at the place on Mondays at four and Sundays at eight am because I have church. No later." Mr. King went back inside and came out with Kayla. She was still passed out from the "surgery" so he placed Kayla into my arms.

"Mr. King!" I said. He knew what would happen if he placed her into my arms.

"This is the beginning of being able to contain your powers. You will feel sick, but work through it. Walk Kayla back to her room." Mr. King had been way off when he said I would feel sick. This was more painful than I could have imagined. Although only some of Kayla's skin was touching me, I still felt the impact.

Dustin awoke and questioned what was going on. I was astonished by what I just heard. I knew and understood everything, but one thing was for sure that I didn't know, and that was whether to tell Kayla or not.

Chapter 13

I opened the door and put her on the bed stroking her hair. As I walked out of the room I started a conversation with Dustin. "So how are things with Gabby?"

"Look, I'm sorry about everything," we said at the same time. We both grinned.

"It's ok, you don't see it, I don't blame you. It's hard to believe me over something as crazy as this. I wouldn't even trust myself either, but its real and it's happening and you're my best friend."

I could see in his eyes he was happy with my reaction toward everything he'd done to me.

"Ok, so now that we're done with that, Gabby is great. We have been on a few dates and I think I'm going to ask her to be my girlfriend."

"That's great," I replied. "Now listen, you can't tell anyone. This is serious and Carter doesn't even know. First, I don't know why you can't see it. Second, I don't know how I got this 'power' in the first place."

'Yeah, I got I-."

"No, you don't. I'm serious," I chopped back before he could finish his sentence.

"Yeah, I got it. Don't worry. I understand. Well, I got to go, but I'll talk to you later." We were in front of my room and he slipped away with no further conversation.

Chapter 14

I woke up from my sleep and tried to comprehend all that happened yesterday. I looked at the alarm clock.

7:45 a.m.

I got up from the bed and quickly put on my clothes. Looking to the side, I saw Carter on his phone, and from the way he was smirking, he was probably talking to one of his girls. "Where are you going at eight in the morning?"

"It's nothing." I put my coat on and raced out the door.

I found my way into the woods. Sitting near the tree in the shade was Mr. King with a bag. "Right on time," he said in a weirdly happy voice.

"Well, I rushed here," I said, taking deep long breaths. "A kid's gotta eat too."

"So here's the start of your training. You need to learn how to control your powers. There are so many things you can do with them."

"Like what?" I didn't know what he was talking about. All I knew was, I was stuck with this weird power and I felt nauseous no matter who touched me.

"What about healing people?" he asked. I forgot

about that. It had been so long since all of that has happened.

"Oh yeah, that too, I guess," I replied.

"Well, you can also feel what other people are feeling. But in order to accomplish that you need to get past the dizziness."

"Is there any way I can stop the spark from appearing?" I asked. I still hadn't figured out why people couldn't see my powers.

"Are you joking? The spark is the best part." He made me sound like I was crazy; like who would want to give up these amazing powers? Well, we'll see how amazing they are. "Now take this." He reached into his bag and pulled out a hard looking rubber ball.

"And what will I use that for?"

"Just hold it." Mr. King sighed. He tossed the ball over to me and I held it in the palm of my hands. Mr. King walked over to me and touched me on the back.

My hands shot out and I began to feel the terrible sensation. I was gagging up spit from being so dizzy and I demanded he let go, so he did.

"You could have warned me!" I said, reaching for air.

"I could have, but I didn't. Grab and squeeze the ball. Put all your frustration and sickness into it. Alright, do it, Kody, do it."

I tried to be brave.

He put his hands on my back. I felt the anger and fatigue of trying to control something that, to me, had no reins. I wanted to scream and let my body take me over because this hurt more than the other times, but I followed Mr. King's instructions. I put my hands on the ball and started pushing the rubber around, trying to manipulate it with my strength and uncontrollable mixed emotions.

Then something changed. I no longer felt the unbearable nausea or anger inside of me. I felt the presence of loss and confusion. I looked at the sparks and it was pure brightness to my eyes.

Mr. King took his hands off and smiled. "You felt it, didn't you."

"I did. It felt weird," I replied.

"And what were you feeling?" he asked.

"Loneliness and confusion. I looked at him and his eyes wandered off. "Are you okay?"

I took a seat on the green grass by the shaded tree and Mr. King followed. He took a deep breath.

"Sometimes. My wife passed away. We were happy living in Canada, married almost for two years. A day after my birthday, she blacked out, forever. We didn't know what it was at first, but then the doctors reported back and said it was cancer. I almost lost it, but she didn't. She made the most out of everything, tried to have me do every little thing she wanted to do. I couldn't keep up and at the same time I couldn't go ahead. I kept my emotions inside; wanting to plan a funeral and ask her where she wanted to be buried, but after I asked she made it seem like the question never came up. Few weeks later I came home from work and there she was on the bed comfortable, wrapped in a blanket. I was going to call the ambulance, but I knew she was happy and wouldn't want me worrying about her forever.

"Then what is confusing about it?" I asked.

"Well, the doctors said her disease wasn't going to kick in until six months later. They had done tests and everything one could think of, but they were wrong and I was crushed. From that day on I didn't know what it was. It didn't make sense. Maybe bad luck. I just don't know. So after a while, I came here looking to be a teacher, and I met Kayla's father and discovered his powers just like yours. You remind me of him."

I didn't know Mr. King had this much to his life. I thought it was just working and sleeping in a repeating cycle. But once I heard everything I really noticed and understood. It wasn't like I *knew* the situation, but it was somewhat related to my dad and mother.

I sighed in overwhelming emotion, realizing everything that had happened. I felt tired and lay my head on the grass. It wasn't like my bed, but it would work.

I heard the sound of the whistle. "Wake up, Wake up!" He kept shouting until I was wide-awake.

"Get up, Kody, we have to continue your training."

What else is there to continue? Didn't I do it? I got up from the grass and walked across to Mr. King. He took a rope and wrapped it around me.

"What *are* you doing to me?"

"Just relax, this is the next step to controlling it," he said. When I pull I want you to use your hands toward me. Now *you* have to use your feelings against the enemy," he said.

"What enemy?" I asked. He ignored the question, ripped the cord, and started pulling me toward him.

At first I gave in, then he started screaming at me: "Use your hands! Don't give in!" I looked at my hands and noticed what I was feeling inside. Time seemed to move so slowly that I almost thought I was on a cloud drifting until I finally landed in a meaning of nowhere. I didn't know how to make the spark appear if no one was touching me, but I focused.

I felt love, immunity and confidence when I was around Kayla, but then the thought of horror surrounded me. I pointed my hands at Mr. King and felt the rush. The lights flashed out and thirty seconds later, Mr. King was on the ground coughing.

"What did I just do?" I asked. He got up from the ground and dusted his hands.

"You did it. You found the inner emotion and let it out. In the beginning I didn't know you'd be able to do that, but the spark in your eye twinkled just before you let the sparks flash out."

"Did Kayla's dad have that?" I asked.

"Yes, so when I saw it on you, I knew you were going to be able to do it."

Mr. King looked at his watch and noticed it was past training hour. "I have to go. I will see you back here tomorrow."

He walked off with his training bag and to my surprise buried it in the secret tree. Before he left he gave me one last look. "I'm also going to need the box back." Before I could reply, he was already out of sight. I sat down and wondered one thing.

"Why was he helping me?"

Chapter 15

I realized I had been asleep for the whole night, I guess no one really knew I was missing because they didn't come out looking for me. It didn't hurt my feelings...much.

The soft grass felt like a pillow, but it itched my skin and I hadn't stopped scratching all morning. For once, it was nice to be away from everything, out in the open. I felt like a part of nature; I could understand what it was trying to tell me by the way the wind blew and the leaves fell on the ground. I walked back to my dorm room to get ready for school. I took off my clothes and headed into the shower. It was all peace and quiet without Carter blasting his music at 7:30 in the morning before school. Then I wondered where he was.

I got out of the shower and texted one of his friends.

Me: Hey, have you seen Carter the past few hours?

Loui: Nope, he told me he was going to a movie, haven't heard from him since.

Something in my gut told me he was in trouble. I looked up the movie theater on my phone and went to Mr. King. He probably would be in his classroom setting up, but he was the only person that knew about me, besides Kayla and Dustin, that had a car.

Without knocking on the door, I rushed in.

He turned around from writing the date on the board. "Why are you here?"

"It's Carter, he hasn't been answering his phone and his friends haven't heard from him since last night. I'm worried about him."

"Where was he?" Mr. King put down the expo marker.

"He was going to a movie." I showed my phone and the location to Mr. King.

"Let's go," Mr. King said, picking up his jacket and car keys. "But first let me do something." He went back to the board and wrote:

Be back in 60 minutes: Talk quietly

We ran into the parking lot to his car, got in and drove to the movie theatre. Even if Carter wasn't picking up for the last thirty minutes I had been trying to contact him, I still didn't give up. I was really worried. Carter usually left me hundreds of messages on my phone that I never got back to.

"We only got sixty minutes, let's check inside the movie theater and then outside in the alley," he said.

Mr. King pulled into the lot. It was completely empty which was good in the case of tracking somebody down, but it made me nervous that Carter could be here.

Carter: I'm in the alley. Come get me please. Carter

I was confused all of the sudden. Carter never ended his text messages with his name at the end. Second, he would always abbreviate as many words as he could. But right now it didn't really matter. My friend was in trouble and I had to do something.

Then I got bumped into the front of the car. I looked in the side mirror and, with little sight, saw blood running down my face. All I could make out was Mr. King grabbing a bottle of water and opening the cap. Mr. King dumped it all over me and the sparks woke me up, kind of like I was being electrocuted.

"Wha.. what happened?" I asked dizzily.

"Someone hit us." Mr. King turned to the back of the car and from the mirror I could only see a silver convertible driving away.

"Why wouldn't they stop and call the police?" Mr. King knew something but the look on his face told me that he wasn't going to tell me.

Then I thought of something that could heal me right away. I put my hands on my face. "Kody, what are you doing? Stop that, you are not ready!"

I heard what Mr. King said, but I was too busy focusing on the healing that I couldn't speak. Sparks appeared throughout my face and I gave a look at Mr. King.

He got his phone out and went to the camera. As he switched the screen I could feel the pain diminishing. It had gone from a slightly massive headache to a screech of a cry.

I looked in the camera of Mr. King's phone and saw the sparks. It was crazy and I didn't even know this could happen. As I didn't know when to stop, I saw electricity in my eyes. They had gone from brown to teal blue and it was a wonderful feeling.

When no more pain was spreading through my body, I took my hands off my face. "Whoa," I said, out of breath.

"How did you do that?" Mr. King asked, putting his phone back into his pocket.

"No time to talk. Now let's go," I said. Mr. King picked a spot and we both got out of the car. We ran to the back alley with Mr. King holding a first aid kit.

It was still bright outside so we could easily find Carter. The closer and closer I got behind the theater, the louder the moan of someone dying on the ground became.

My eyes shot straight ahead. "Follow me."

It was darker in the alley because it was in the back of the theatre that was covered by a large roof.

Mr. King walked behind me toward the boy lying on the ground. "Take out your flashlight." I whispered.

Mr. King turned on the light and there was Carter lying on the ground with blood coming out of his chest. I looked up and saw the shining light before me was gone. "We have to get him to the hospital," Mr. King said dialing 911.

"No time, he's dying." I had never done a heal as big as this one before. I placed my hands on his chest and focused on what Mr. King had taught me in training. I focused on my feelings. The love, the horror, but right now seeing a good friend alive. The bloody image was a gruesome sight but became less so as my hands started to heal him. I could hear Carter start breathing normally again and I glanced at Mr. King with an expression of relief. Then one thing slowed me down causing me to look at my bloody hands; one more person finding out my deepest darkest secret.

Chapter 16

"Get him off the ground," Mr. King said.

"I can't." I moved away to let Mr. King pick Carter off the ground. I thought it was going to be hard for him, but it looked very easy. Mr. King just lifted him up without any trouble. But the blood was getting all over Mr. King and he looked worried. "Ew." The smell of blood shocked me. I didn't even know there was a smell. "We gotta go."

With blood seeping into his clothes, Mr. King started running to the car. I was almost paralyzed. I didn't think something like this happened in Denmark. I mean it was one of the safest towns.

Although I healed Carter enough for him to breathe, it was obvious he was shot and needed assistance. I was really scared because I didn't want to tell anyone about my powers.

We walked casually to the nurse's office, but before we walked in, Mr. King stopped me. "Kody, I know this is a big secret and I don't blame you for wanting it to stay that way. However, we need a nurse on our side."

For some reason, I knew he was right. We needed a person who was good with health and could help us in further situations.

"Alright, but which one?" I peeked through the window seeing all five nurses helping out students.

Mr. King pointed to a girl with a high blonde bun wearing funky shoes and makeup. Over her uniform she had a panda pin and her cup size was massive, although she was fit. I wasn't sure if Mr. King was losing it or just desperate. "Are you sure? What's her name?" I asked.

"Amanda--she looks sloppy, but she is actually very smart. She just dresses like that to impress people."

"For boys," I said with a slight cough.

He gave me a sly look.

"Fine, but I'm not talking." Mr. King opened the door and headed in before me.

"Help, Amanda, please!" Right away she turned and headed to him.

"What's wrong, Jason?" she asked, taking him into her arms. Surprisingly, Amanda was very strong. With her mismatched clothes and incredibly high heeled shoes, I wasn't sure she was a real nurse. How could she be taken seriously in that kind of outfit?

Mr. King gave me a look, and I nodded in response.

He walked forward to Amanda, grabbed her on the arm, and started to pull her outside. "Where are we going?" Amanda said, squealing.

Mr. King looked both ways and made sure no one was around. It was all coming back to me at the same time. The feeling where everything changes for you, I was hearing it again, but instead this time it wasn't to me.

"I'm about to tell you something crazy, but you're going to need to believe me, sis," he said.

What? Did he just say sister?

"What is it, Jason?" She reached out to touch his hands. She looked over to me. "Who is this?"

"This is Kody and he has the same thing as Kayla's dad, Ronnie."

"What? How can that be? It only happens like every century." Amanda let go of Mr. King's hands and walked my way. I backed away from her. "What a handsome young boy? Are you a model?"

My cheeks blushed and I began to feel hot. "No."

"Amanda!" Mr. King shouted.

"Sorry, Sorry, so Kody has the 'power'," Amanda said, putting her hands up in quotation marks.

"Yes, and the guy in the office we brought in, was shot," Mr. King said.

"By whom?" she asked.

"We don't know."

"Mr. King? Do you think it was an accident?" I interrupted the conversation.

"We both know that was no accident." He gave me a look of empathy, but also glimpsed a flash of anger.

Chapter 17

"But why would someone do that?" The blood was rushing to my face and I could feel the anger rise in me. It just didn't make sense. Who was evil enough to do this?

I stopped talking and listened to the conversation Mr. King and Amanda were having. "I can't do it, stuff like this doesn't happen for a nurse to take on. Carter needs to go to the hospital," Amanda said, looking back at the window.

I could see Mr. King was worried. There was sweat dripping down his face and his hands were shaking. "Remember what happened last time with Ronnie and the guy?" Mr. King said.

"Yes, I do, but we know what to say now and they can take care of Carter much better than we can," Amanda said enforcing the idea.

"Alright then."

Amanda opened the door, took the phone and called 911.

"Hi, this is Amanda at the Pinewoods Academy, we have a student here who was just shot, we need help."

I went to the bathroom to wash my hands off. I took the soap, spread it all over my bloody hands, and counted to ten. The sparks appeared, but they didn't hurt as much so I guess Mr. King's training was helping.

I came out of the bathroom and walked over to the bed where Carter lay unconscious. When I came back to the room, he wasn't there. A strip of blood stained his empty bed. "Mr. King?" I called out.

A nurse came over to me. "Sorry, he's not here anymore, think he left with Amanda."

"Great," I murmured under my breath. I didn't know what to do now. My friend was gone and it was Monday morning. I headed out the door and went back to my room to get changed and grab my work. I literally just threw something on and ran to my classroom because I was already late.

"You're late," said the teacher. I didn't know who she was, probably a fill-in because Mr. King went to the hospital. She was short. Had long black hair and wore no makeup. Her shoes were hot pink and her dress was flowy with dots; she wore black glasses. She was actually pretty.

"Who are you?" I asked, trying not to sound rude. Everyone stopped and turned their heads towards me.

"I'm the fill-in teacher, Mrs. Pearl." She looked at me and pulled down her black glasses. I walked to my seat, opened my writing book and started drawing the eye that Kayla drew when I first saw her.

It was about thirty minutes into the class when the

phone rang. "Yes, yes he is." I knew that was me and so I got up. "Well, Kody, seems like you know where to go." I ran down the hallway to the nurse's office, where I saw Mr. King sitting next to Carter.

"How is he?" I asked.

"Fine, they were able to remove the bullet easily and he was given a few stitches. It was impressive how well you healed him, but it wasn't enough to remove the bullet." I looked at his wound, still slowly oozing all over his shirt.

"Is this even gonna work!" I put my hands over my head and felt the hot temperature clouding up my head. I was about to feel sick to my stomach. I ran to the other side through the door with Mr. King following me. I threw up and lay down on the floor.

"What is happening?" I asked Mr. King.

"I think you're getting sick from not absorbing feelings; that's what happened to Kayla's father."

"Mr. King?" I stood up.

"Yes?" he looked at me.

"Is Carter going to be okay?"

He gave me a stare.

"No."

Chapter 18

"Are you joking?" I can't lose my roommate. Not another let-down. Why was this happening to me? I didn't ask to be caught in something like this.

"Kody, we will figure it out, I promise-"

"But why do you say he won't live?" I asked.

He reached into his pockets and pulled out a bullet. It was bright silver with an arm design. It didn't look like a regular bullet. It had a pointy top and flat surface. The point had dry blood marks from the sharp shot. " I asked for this after the doctors took it out. I don't know what it means--we're going to go to the library tomorrow. But this is bad. Someone knows about you, and I don't know who."

I dropped on the floor again and felt my head hit the concrete.

"Kody, be ready, I'm going to put your hand on my hand. Remember what I told you about controlling it. Think of the good you have in your life." I thought about my mom, the way she'd always pack pink-flavored bubble gum, hoping I would give it to a girl one day, Maybe *today* was the day. Then I thought about a future with Kayla . How this was meant to be? Coming to school, meeting her, falling in love. *Wait, what? Am I in love? I mean I think I am I just thought it.*

"Kody, now!" He put his arm on my hand and I focused deeply, sucking the feelings out of him. I pushed away the sickness and ignored the anger that built up. My eyes were closed the whole time, but I knew we were still touching hands because of the way I felt. My body began to act up. I gained more energy, yet my feelings had altered. Mr. King pulled his hand off and stood up while I remained lying on the floor.

"Are you ok?" he asked. I didn't know what I was feeling.

"I think so, although I feel worried--scared about something, but I don't know what." Then it came to me. These were Mr. King's feelings and they were about Carter. It didn't feel so good having his feelings in my body. I was worried, but not like he was. I got up and ran inside to see Carter.

"Carter, Carter!" I was yelling at him to wake up. I just couldn't see him die right in front of me. Mr. King came running back and took my arms and held them behind my back. I kept calling his name and the faces of people in the nurse's office looked my way.

I looked back at Carter and blacked out.

I woke up in my bed with Kayla sitting next to me. "Hey." I sat up from my bed.

"What happened?" I said, feeling my head.

"You were disrupting the nurse's office and Mr. King pulled your arms behind you. I guess you weren't ready for that. Then you blacked out. Nobody saw." I sighed and fell back on my bed.

"Can I lie down with you?" asked Kayla. I wanted to say yes so badly, but I didn't know what would happen. But I didn't want something like this to ruin our relationship. I was going to focus and just breathe.

I opened my arms for Kayla and she came into bed with me. We pulled the comforters over and snuggled together. I breathed in and out. *Sparks don't appear, sparks don't appear,* I kept saying to myself with my eyes closed. Kayla turned to me "Kody, open your eyes." So I did. "There are no sparks!"

"Wait, let me try something. Sparks appear," I said. The sparks appeared through my hands with a shining bright light. I looked at Kayla and was so happy. I could finally control my powers. Without saying the words, I thought them and the sparks disappeared.

"I knew you could do it." Kayla turned to face me and moved closer. I felt her warm cheek hit my neck and then I could tell what she was feeling. Love. I smiled and looked into her eyes.

"Kayla, I love you."

My heart raced and I began to feel embarrassed. We still looked at each other and she had a smile on her face.

"I love you too, Kody." I leaned in to kiss her. After we broke apart, I realized the sparks hadn't appeared that time either. I put my hand on her cheek and leaned in again. This time it was faster and more moving of side-to-side. I loved her so much that I didn't care about anything. I didn't judge her in any sort of way. "Kody?"

"Yeah," I asked, kissing the side of her neck.

"I want this, but not now."

I stopped kissing her. When she said that I felt some sort of confidence. How she wanted this, and so did I, but not now. It was too early and we were only in 9th grade. I didn't want to rush anything because I knew she liked me. A lot of my friends had been more experienced than me. Yeah, I grew up in a nasty neighborhood, but my mom was there to guide me and help me throughout the way.

I looked into her eyes. "I feel the same way." Kayla turned around and I lay on my stomach. I put my hand over her and silence was music to my ears.

"Just set him down," I heard someone whisper. I woke up with my arms still wrapped around Kayla. Mr. King turned and came over to my bed while Amanda lay next to Carter.

"It's not what it looks like."

"Don't worry, I'm not gonna tell anyone. I think

it's cute. Good job controlling your powers." I rolled my eyes at him, but I knew he didn't care. I got up and walked over to Carter's bed. I had tried to talk to Carter earlier in the nurse's office, but I was too crazy then. I walked over to Amanda. "How is he now?"

"Still the same, but we have to keep hoping." I watched Carter on his bed, covered up with bandages and ice packs. His face was pale and had a big streak of dried blood on his lip. I lifted up his shirt without Amanda's permission. She did not say a word. I looked closer and saw the bullet hole. It was filled with pus and a gruesome expression hit my face. I wanted to look away. But something pulled me to look. I felt sorry for him.

"Who would shoot a kid?" She didn't answer my question.

"I'm going to go now. I will check up on him." Amanda got up from the bed and headed to the door.

"What day is it?" I asked.

She turned around. "Tuesday, goin' on Wednesday." I got up from Carter's bed and walked over to Kayla. Instead of waking her up to go back to her dorm, I let her sleep, hoping her comfort could prepare me for tomorrow, if there was anything to happen.

Chapter 19

Buzz-Buzz. My phone vibrated right next to me and I put my hand under the blanket to grab it. It was a text from Mr. King.

Mr. King: How is Carter? I will cover for you and Kayla.

Nothing happened yesterday that was important. Carter was still in bed and Kayla slept over again. I poked my head up from the pillow and saw Carter there, playing on his phone. He looked okay, then I texted Mr. King back.

Me: He is fine, playing on his phone and thanks

I sent the message, but then I realized it was a big deal—Carter was playing on his phone!

"Kayla, wake up!" I kept shaking her, knowing to block the spark. She woke up and looked at me.

"What? Are we going to be late for class?"

"Look at Carter," I said to her, pointing to Carter's bed. She got up and walked over to him.

"Carter! How are you feeling?" she asked.

"I'm fine," Carter said. Kayla put her hands softly around his body and gave him a hug.

"You don't want to touch me."

"Ouch," said Kayla, pulling back after the hug. Her

arm was red and she looked paler. "I feel.... tired." Kayla yawned.

"What did you do to her?" I said, pulling Carter's shirt.

"Don't touch my hands, freak," he said in a snotty voice.

I instantly removed my hands and turned to Kayla who was on the floor sitting and looking at her hand that was bright red. She looked at me confusedly and tested her strength to stand back up.

"What did you just say?" Kayla asked.

"You heard me, you hand freak." I knew Carter was obnoxious, but why was he acting like this? How'd he find out about my power? Mr. King and I were with him the whole time so when would he have found out? Except....when he was shot. Could the person or people have told him? What if they shot him, then told more people? All this time I knew this could be a disaster waiting to happen.

I looked at my phone and Mr. King was calling me. "Well, I got to go," said Carter throwing back the sheets of his bed and combing his hair with gel. Oddly, he was already dressed.

"Hello?"

"Hi Kody, how is Carter?" asked Mr. King. By the time I could answer, Carter was out the door and Kayla was icing her arm. "Hello?"

"Yeah, Hi. He's gone. It was really weird. He acted like nothing had happened," I said.

"I'm coming as fast as I can," Mr. King said. Then he hung up. I put my phone on my bed and walked over to Kayla, who was now looking at the mirror. She kept touching her arm, which looked scarred.

"Are you okay?" I asked. I was reaching to touch her arm, when her hands met mine. "No, don't. I don't want it."

"That is a pretty big scar, I'm not gonna let you live with that."

"Fine, but this is the last time." I knew Kayla was serious, but it was my duty to protect her and although she wanted to suffer and feel the pain like a normal human, it wasn't so. She had a meta-human boyfriend and Kayla had to deal with that whether she liked it or not. I placed my hands on her scar. *Sparks, appear.* The sparks appeared, but the scar wasn't going away. "Why isn't it working?" Kayla asked.

"I don't know." I was sure that my power could heal; it did last time.

"Kody, Stop. You're hurting me," Kayla said as my hands were still producing electricity while I touched her hands. Then, after a few seconds I let go.

"I don't understand why it's not working." Then I heard the knock on the door.

"Open up, it's Mr. King." I walked over and opened

the door. He looked at the bed and then at me. "Where did he go?" I had never seen Mr. King more worried in my entire life. There were veins pulsing down his head and there was a concerned look on his face. His hands were over his head and he looked like he was going to pass out. Mr. King sat on Carter's bed and felt the sheets. "I think something is wrong."

"Duh," I said. Mr. King looked at me, but held in his anger.

"No, I'm serious, the bullet I showed you, I've seen it before. It's not a good sign. All I know is it means something bad, but I don't know why Carter was shot."

"What do these people want?" I asked.

"You."

Chapter 20

"Why would they want me?" I asked worriedly.
"Because, they think you're a threat--with your powers and all."

"But I don't hurt anyone! I use them for good," I shouted.

" I don't think they really care."

"So let me get this straight. Me, the fifteen-year-old boy, is getting followed by these people because I'm 'dangerous' and they're jealous of me?"

"Correct."

"So what we gonna do?"

"Get the one thing they want most, besides you," Mr. King said.

"The box?"

"Yes. Now where is it?" I was unsure if trusting Mr. King was a good idea. I mean he was helping, but something didn't seem right. What was he going to do with the box?

"Uhh, I hid it in my closet." Mr. King got up and went to the closet. He looked through all my clothes and threw stuff on the ground.

"Where is it, Kody, I need it now." Mr. King walked to me and was talking in my face. He was becoming angry. I almost tripped on clothes behind me because Mr. King was poking me in the chest pushing me back. "Kody, I need it."

I protested back. "For what?!"

"You don't understand, do you?"

"Understand what?" I asked impatiently.

"With Kayla's dad. He found the box, we tried to get it open and find out what was inside of it, but we couldn't find the key. And suddenly it was too late, Ronnie was dead and the box was gone. I never knew who took it until you found it."

"Why would it have my father's name under it, though?"

"That's what I'm trying to figure out. It's not safe for you to have it. Especially now that the people know it's you." I went under my bed and took the box out. I handed it to Mr. King who took his time looking at it. His hands felt the sides of the box while dusting off the remaining dirt. Kayla walked over to me and slapped me in the face."

"What did you do that f-."

"You know exactly why. How could you not tell me?" Then I knew what she was talking about: Ronnie, her father. The look in her eyes made me weak. I had nothing to say that I knew would make her feel better. She walked over to my bed and put her knees to her head. I heard a sniffle or two and I thought, *what have I done?* All this was just to protect her. I walked over to my bed and started to rub her back. Fortunately, she didn't lean back or knock my hands off.

"You know I just did it to protect you. I didn't know how to react and you know I have never lied to you. I would have told you, but I didn't want to see you upset."

"I know, I just can't believe my own father would keep this from me."

"I think he was just trying to protect you from the truth."

"What truth?" Kayla said.

"Well, that's what we're trying to figure out. You heard that these people are after me. They also shot Carter, but I don't know what happened to your father and now I am telling you the truth."

Kayla uncurled her body and gave me a hug. Her warm neck brushed mine once again and I felt her sadness. I wanted to give her happiness, but I felt like I couldn't give that to her.

"Okay guys, now that that's over, can you go find Carter? I'm going to see if I can open the box with whatever I can find." That didn't sound too convincing to me. But I didn't argue. I took Kayla's hand and walked outside the door.

"Text me if you find anything," Mr. King said.

We walked around the boys' dorm room and went from door to door. People were saying all kinds of things like, "Saw him in the library" or "He went swimming in the pool." I didn't know what to believe. I know Mr. King told me to go find Carter with Kayla, but there were so many places where he could be. I thought of going into the woods with Kayla and showing her what I learned.

"Let's go to the woods, I need to show you something," I said.

"What?" she asked.

We moved side by side, running together in the wind to the woods. It was an amazing feeling with the wind blowing in our faces. It was like one of those movies where the couples are running together in slow motion. It was cheesy, but it felt like that.

"What do you want to show me?"

I gently touched Kayla to guide her to the tree.

"Just stay back and don't come near me until I say so." I walked to another tree on an angle where Kayla could see me.

"Kody?" Kayla sounded worried.

I focused deeply. Putting my hands out in front of me, I looked at Kayla and then down at the ground. In my mind I thought, *sparks appear.* I felt the adrenaline kick through my body. I felt the sparks coming through. The sparks flashed out of my hands. It hurt so much, there was agonizing pain that took all of my strength to release the powers. It's not that I was becoming weak, I was just using more energy than I had ever used before—besides the time in the car. "Ughhh," I yelled.

"Kody!" Everything was so blurry. Again and again it hurt. I felt it; I needed to control it. *Come on, Kody, you got this.* Then, I did it.

"Kody," Kayla kept yelling. From the corner of my eye I saw Kayla walking toward me.

"No." My voice changed. It was suddenly lower. I looked up at her and somehow I could see a reflection of myself in her face. My eyes were strikingly blue and there was electrcity in them. Kayla covered her mouth with her hands and backed up. I looked at the tree and thrust my hands out. The sparks stung the tree and I kept pushing and pushing them harder. "Ahh." It still hurt, but it felt good, like a release of some sort. I controlled myself for the sparks to come to an end. The flash disappeared and the sparks died down.

I looked at Kayla who was looking at the tree that now had a hole through it. "Wow kid, you're strong." I smiled, thankful she responded that way. The last thing I wanted to do was scare her off, but Kayla wasn't like that and that's another reason why I loved her. She walked toward me and I grabbed her hands. Kayla's hand went up to my face and she gasped.

"What?" I asked.

She grabbed a mirror out of her bag quickly and I looked at it. Then I knew what she was talking about; there was a spark in my eye like Mr. King told me before, but I was surprised she hadn't noticed it sooner. Kayla put back the mirror when I received a text. I took my phone out of my pocket.

Mr. King: Better come down here, Dustin not so good. I don't know what happened just saw him with a black eye.

Me: Okay, thanks. Where are you now?

Mr. King: I know I said I would try to find the key, but I'm reading over the newspaper from the day Kayla's dad died.

Me: I thought you said he committed suicide.

Mr. King: Like I said, I'm sure that didn't happen.

"Who is that?" Kayla asked. I was going to tell her the truth because not telling her could ruin everything again. I mean almost ruin everything.

"Mr. King is looking at news from the day your father died," I said.

"What's to look at, he committed suicide," Kayla said walking away toward the tree.

"Mr. King thinks your dad was murdered."

Kayla suddenly stopped and looked at me—a death look grew upon her soft face.

Chapter 21

"Why does he think so?" she asked, laying her head against the tree. I walked to her, laid my hands around her waist and her head went onto my chest, slightly touching the skin. I closed my eyes and I felt the sadness inside of her, but then I felt worry.

"Why are you worried?" I asked.

"Because, I know my father didn't commit suicide."

"When did you start to think this?" I asked her.

"When I met you." She lifted her head and turned it around to me. I leaned in for a kiss and she responded by kissing back.

Mr. King: Now Kody!

Me: Sorry, sorry, coming.

I put my phone away. "We have to go now, there is something wrong with Dustin." We ran back together to the nurse's office in no more than five minutes.

When we got to the office, Dustin was on a nurse bed with a patch over his eye. Dustin had a book in his hands titled: Ancestry.

Kayla and I walked over to the bed and tapped Dustin on the shoulder. "Hey buddy." I said, taking my hand off. Dustin lifted the eye patch and looked at me.

"Eww...... I'm sorry, that was jerky." I said apologetic.

"Whatever, I'll get over it," Dustin said putting the eye patch on the side of his bed.

"So, what happened? Who did this and why?"

"Well, I was in the library reading this book." Dustin lifted the book up and put it back down. "Then a couple of seconds later, Carter walks in."

"Wait, Carter?" I asked.

"Yes, I looked back at him and said 'hey.' He didn't respond so I looked back at the book. Carter walked closer and I saw him look at the paper when I turned the page. He grabbed the book from me, so I grabbed it back. He hit me in the face and knocked me off the chair. I saw Carter take a picture of the page and walk off."

"What was the page?" Kayla asked. Dustin sat up slowly and started opening the book. He turned about 50 pages in and showed the page to us. The picture was scratched on the outside like people had been fighting for it. I looked in the middle of the page and saw this big evil eye necklace.

"O-M-G," were just the words that came out of Kayla's mouth. I turned to her.

"What? Do you recognize that?" I said to her.

"My father gave it to me, before he died."

Chapter 22

Dustin and I shared a quick glance. He closed the book and put it back on his lap. "Where is it?" I asked.

"It's in safekeeping, but I'll get it later," Kayla said.

"By the way, how did you touch me without, ya know?" Dustin asked.

"Yeah, I know you can't see it, but anyway I controlled it. But I wanna do something," I said to Dustin. I put my hands on his face.

"You're not gonna kiss me are you?" he asked.

"Duh no," Kayla interrupted. I was going to open my mouth, but it was like she knew exactly what I was going to say. Kayla walked over to the other side of Dustin, blocking the view from the nurses seeing anything suspicious.

"What are you doing?" Dustin asked.

"Just wait, I told you before, didn't I?" I closed my hands and focused on the sparks going through a cord in my body to Dustin's. I opened my eyes and Kayla turned my way. Dustin's eye was fully healed. There was no black or purple surrounding his eye; it was like nothing happened.

All of the sudden Mr. King came our way over to the bed.

"Good job Kody."

"Could my father ever do that?" Kayla asked, reluctant to hear the answer.

"No, I don't think he had what Kody has."

"And what is that?" asked Dustin.

"Wisdom."

"Wait, the homework, you assigned us. The one with the touch…"

"Yes, I did that on purpose. I don't know if I mentioned that to you. The day you walked into class and shook my hand I knew you had it. As I said before, you had the spark in your eye.

"But why me?" I asked.

"I'm still trying to figure that out too," Mr. King said, sitting down on the chair.

"And my father," asked Kayla.

"Him too, didn't know either."

"Who is the girl in the book then?" asked Dustin. Mr. King looked to Dustin.

"Still don't know that either."

'There's a lot of things you don't know," I said.

"I'm doing the best I can, aren't I?" Mr. King stammered back. "I helped you control your powers, open your eyes to everything, and have shown you that your powers can heal people. Kody, you have a gift."

I was actually the one who discovered the healing part of my powers, but I kept that comment to myself. "I know and thank you." I looked at my hands in front of me. And then I made the sparks appear.

"Kody, put those away," Mr. King said, standing up.

So I did. I know that I didn't want anyone finding out my secret anymore, but right now I didn't care. There was another question on my mind.

"Why did Carter want that?" I asked Mr. King.

"I don't know but we're going to find out."

Then the nurse came over to the area and pushed Kayla out of the way.

"What is going on in here?" she demanded.

"Nothing miss," Mr. King replied.

She walked away and I could tell she rolled her eyes. Then I remembered something. Carter touched him. Then I had a flashback to when Kayla touched Carter for a hug.

"Dustin… Did Carter touch you anywhere else besides your eye?" I asked.

He looked around his body. "No, I don't think so," he said putting his hand down.

"Wait. Dustin, give me your hand."

Dustin put out his hand for me. I looked around his wrist and saw a scar. Then I remembered when Kayla got touched by Dustin and got a scar. "Mr. King, look at this." Mr. King took Dustin's wrist and felt the scar.

"And you're sure you could only have gotten this by Carter touching you?" Mr. King asked, still looking at the wrist.

"Yeah, I haven't realized it before now." Dustin said as Mr. King let go of his wrist.

"Let me see, Dustin," Mr. King asked again. "Kayla, come over here too." Mr. King grabbed both of their hands and turned their wrists. There were two scars; same length--looked exactly the same.

"What does this mean?" I asked.

"I don't know, but I do think Carter getting shot affected his personality," Mr. King said.

"He also healed right away which didn't make sense. I mean you saw it, Kody. He was so bad for the two nights and then the next morning he was fine." I agreed with what Kayla was saying. This all didn't make sense again.

"Where did you put the box?" I asked Mr. King.

"Don't worry, it's safe." By meaning safe, I was guessing it was hidden somewhere in his classroom.

"Now Kody, let's leave Dustin here. We are going to go to the library and find out what this bullet means." Mr. King pulled the bullet out and covered it with his hands.

"Don't drop it," I said.

"I'll go get the necklace," Kayla said. "Call you when I have it."

I said ok and went on walking with Mr. King through the doorway.

While walking, Mr. King began to talk. "So I see you and Kayla are pretty close.

"Yeah we are, I love her."

"Meaning that…have you?"

"No! And not to be mean but that is none of your business."

"Kody, you know I'm not trying to be weird, but I am the closest thing you have to a father and I just want to protect you." I felt weird hearing that from an older male, especially someone who reminded me so much of my father.

"I know and thanks, but we decided we're not going to do it this year."

"Good, I'm glad to hear that, but you know if you need anything or have any questions I'm here for you," Mr. King said when we entered the library.

"OK. Ok……" We walked to the front desk. "I got it, Mr. King, let me ask. Do you have any sections on bullet info?" I asked.

"Who says info?" Mr. King replied to me.

"I do, but why the hell does that matter?" I said, rolling my eyes.

"Yes hon, we do. Second section on your right." I walked with Mr. King to the section.

"So where is it?" I asked. Mr. King put his hand on the book- shelf and started to run his hand across it. He closed his eyes. "Why are you closing your eyes?" I asked. Like that wasn't stupid enough.

"Got it." He opened his eyes and grabbed the book.

"How do you know it's right?" I asked. Mr. King turned and I noticed the title was:

Bullets

What? How did he know? "There is something you're not telling me."

"And what would that be?" Mr. King said, almost laughing at me.

"Well, first you find the right book with your eyes closed, then you say you 'followed' me and Kayla into the woods. And somehow I feel like you knew I was coming with Kayla and Dustin."

He looked up from reading the book. "Well, aren't you smart. Seriously." Mr. King got up from the desk. "It's amazing how your brain works. Kayla's father never found out, I had to tell him myself."

"Tell him what?" I asked.

"Well, what do you think? You think something is fishy, so what is it? he asked.

I had to think about this for a second. There was no evidence that he had my powers because Mr. King couldn't do the things that I could. He couldn't be a vampire because he would want my blood nor a werewolf or else he would turn every time he got really frustrated (which was a lot). I thought about a fairy, but what could that have to do with anything? Then a merman crossed my mind but that didn't make sense either. Then it came to me. There was no *name* for it.

"Locator," I mumbled.

"Kody, you got it. You did it," he said happily.

"So you can tell where people are?" I asked.

"Yes, well only when I want to." It was hard to believe Mr. King, so I was going to test him.

"Then where is Kayla?" I asked.

"Give me your hand before you ask why. I need something that relates to the person so I can eventually connect." So I gave him my hand. Mr. King closed his eyes. Five seconds later Mr. King said, "She's in her room, but just came back from the cafeteria. Probably looking."

In order to see if Mr. King was right I texted Kayla.

Me: Where are you?

Kayla: In room, I must have put the necklace somewhere else everything ok?

Me: Yeah sorry, text me if you find it.

Kayla: kk

So it was true. He could really locate where people were. "Well, we haven't got all day." Mr. King said, sitting down in the chair. I sat down hoping this wouldn't take forever because honestly I have a life, but then I thought more clearly--this is my life.

Chapter 23

"What are we exactly looking for?" I asked. I looked at the bullet and searched through more pages. I found nothing. It was all stuff on how to make a bullet, what kind of bullets, but no signs whatsoever.

"I think I found it," Mr. King said. I got up from my seat and went over to see the other book. "It says here that this bullet is only found in special places and only used by Polymortons."

"What the heck is that?" I asked.

"Hold on," Mr. King said as he lowered his hands to the bottom of the page. "The arm symbol…. it means "to claim," Mr. King said, looking at me.

"Claim what, though?" I had no idea what the symbol meant. All I knew was right then and there that I was looking at a page with a type of bullet.

"Maybe you," Mr. King said softly. I knew I had heard something like "yew" come out of Mr. King's mouth, but I wasn't too sure.

"What did you say?" I asked, going back to my seat across from the table.

"Maybe they are trying to say that they want you for something, how they are threatened or something. I don't know. I tried figuring it out with Ronnie, but we never got the chance to finish it." Mr. King pulled out his phone and took a picture of the page.

Suddenly, my phone began to ring and it was Kayla; I picked up the call talking quietly.

"Hey, so I found the necklace, but I can't open the locket."

"How come?"

"It's like dusty and it's like someone glued this thing."

"Shi-"

"Kody!" Mr. King said, putting the book away.

"What?" I knew what he was talking about, but I was a teenager and there wasn't a law saying I couldn't curse, but Carter must have gotten into Kayla's room and glued the necklace. Who else could it be? The only one acting strange was Carter.

"Well, let's go and check it out." I ran next to Mr. King in the hallway. Both of us were, almost knocking people down, stepping on their bags and once I even knocked a bottle of water onto someone's face; it was pretty funny.

Mr. King knocked on Kayla's door. "What happens if Carter actually messed it up?" I asked.

"Well, first we don't know if that happened and if it did then we would have to un-glue it." Kayla opened the door and pulled both our hands in. "Why are you pulling us?" I asked her.

"Look at this." Kayla placed the necklace in front of our hands. "I was trying to take the glue off. I put water, alcohol and salt with water and nothing worked. I found tweezers and tried snapping the part open." While Kayla was talking I walked over to the window. I saw people reading, kissing and walking as they were drinking their coffee. "It finally snapped open and guess what I found?"

I turned around and she looked at me. "A camera."

"Let me see." Mr. King reached out to grab the necklace. "You definitely pulled it off." He rotated the necklace and I walked over. "Here it is," he said. "Do you have a magnifying glass?"

Kayla went into her backpack and pulled out a magnifying glass. She handed it to Mr. King when he closed in on a tiny black circle. "Got it."

"Is that the camera?"

"Yes."

"How can someone see us with something that small?" I asked.

"It's not impossible, but very, very hard to accomplish," he said, doubting what he was seeing. "Did anything seem out of place when you got back?"

"Ummm, not really besides this note that was left on my bed from Gabby." I walked over to the bed and picked up the note, reading it aloud.

"Hey girl, meet me in the parking lot around nine, wanna take you somewhere..... This doesn't sound like her."

"That's what I thought too. First, she never wants to surprise me and she always spells the word girl with a U." Suddenly, me and Kalya looked at each other.

"Carter must have written that," Mr. King said, poking his eye into the camera."

"What if Gabby got one that says the same thing?" she asked.

"Call her," I said.

"Gabby? Did you get a note? It's not from me. You need to come over here right now." I couldn't hear anything on the other end of the line.

"Kayla, what is wron--- Ahhhh."

"Gabby? What is wrong? Are you there?"

"What is going on?" I whispered. Kayla had such a worried look on her face, like she had just seen a ghost. "Put it on speaker."

Kayla put her phone outwards. "This is the Polymortons, surrender the stone or she dies."

Chapter 24

The phone hung up and Kayla just stayed still, looking at me. I didn't know what to say to that so I asked Mr. King. "What are we going to do?"

"Right now we have to go back and get the box before they do and call the police."

"They are not answering," I said, confused.

"That is really weird, but never mind that. We have more important things to do."

"Where do you think Carter and Gabby are?" Kayla asked.

"Give me the note, Kody." Mr. King said, sticking out his hand. I handed the note to Mr. King while he closed his eyes and rubbed the note.

"What the heck is he doing?" she asked.

"Just wait," I said to Kayla. Kayla walked over to me. I nodded that it was okay.

"He's........" Mr. King's eyes were still closed, but his face was confused. Mr. King flipped over the note and kept feeling it. His eyes were closed and he walked over to the window. Kayla and I turned around and watched him as he neared the window.

"What is it?" I asked, hoping it wouldn't be as bad as it seemed. I walked to the side of him and left Kayla in her spot. Mr. King opened his eyes and breathed.

"There." Mr. King put down the note and I looked in the direction he was looking. I saw Carter looking on an Ipad then up at the window. Carter knew the whole time where we all were. He'd been there looking through the camera. Carter smiled an evil grin and walked away. I walked over to Mr. King and located the camera.

"You won't get away with this," I said, frustrated.

"Kody, your eyes," Mr. King said as he turned me to face the mirror. I tried to feel calmer. Kayla walked over and hugged me from behind. She knew not to say anything. A few seconds later, I looked into the mirror and my eyes were back to normal brown. Looking back at Mr. King I realized there was no response from Carter.

Then a sort- of microphone went off. "I already have." It was Carter's voice. I tried to find where the voice was coming from. I looked at Mr. King.

"Sorry kid, can't locate that." It felt like Carter or the Polymortons had gotten away with it.

"This is not over yet," Mr. King said. "I will go back to the classroom and get the box. I'll text you asap." Mr. King sprinted out the door and within seconds I couldn't see him.

"Well, what do we do now?" Kayla said, hopelessly dropping down on her bed.

"We find out where Gabby is and bring the

key(necklace) so we can open the box and find out what they want with the stone." Kayla confidently got up from the bed, running out the door. I followed behind her calling her name, but I stopped because I knew where she was going.

"How come you never talk about your mother?" I asked when I caught up to her.

"We don't have time to talk about that," she said. Kayla opened the door to the school and looked at me. "Are you coming?"

While walking quickly in the hallway I pulled out my phone and speed dialed Mr. King.

"Hello?" Mr. King said.

"Hey, have necklace coming to your classroom, do you have the box?" I asked.

"Bad news, can't find it. I'm sure I put it there."

"What is he saying?" said Kayla.

"He can't find the box."

I put back the phone.

"Well, what are we going to do now?" I asked. Then a vibration hit my phone. I looked at it and it had an address.

I stopped right where we were, which was in front of the door.

Number unknown
If you want Gabby, come to this address, alone.
38 Meldrive avenue

"We gotta go," I said to Kayla. We ran to Mr. King's classroom. We opened the door and he was at his desk with his hands over his head. He looked sweaty and there were papers and folders all over the place. There were some keys in front of him and Mr. King looked like he had been searching for ages.

"Don't ask," Mr. King said, taking his hands off his face and looking at the both of us.

"I got a text. I think from the Polymortons. It says the address, maybe the box is there too."

He got up from his desk. "But it says I have to go alone."

"Hell, you're not going alone," Mr. King said, taking his car keys. There it was again. The father-like behavior that made me feel okay. I was happy Mr. King was in this with me; I don't know what I would have done if I couldn't have someone to share it with.

We ran to the car and Mr. King started the engine. "Kayla, watch the back in case anyone sees us leave. We need an excuse since I'm not working. I hired Ms. Pearl to substitute."

"What should I be looking out for?" Kayla asked.

"Cars, anything that looks suspicious," Mr. King replied. He checked his mirrors and pulled the gear in front. Mr. King pulled out his GPS. "What's the address, Kody?"

"38 Meldrive Avenue." Mr. King typed the letters

onto the screen and the programming began. I looked back at Kayla, then to Mr. King. "Let's go."

Mr. King drove out of the parking lot and onto the road. We immediately hit traffic. "This is great," I said sarcastically.

"Don't worry, I have a siren," Mr. King said. I didn't know it was an actual siren when he pulled it out from the glove compartment in front of me. " I have never used it, but got it as a teacher. My dad was also a police officer so he got it for my birthday."

"How old are you?" Kayla asked. We both laughed. Mr. King didn't look old at all. I was guessing this happened about eight years ago so he had to be in his early 30s.

"That doesn't matter now, Kayla!"

"I'm sorry. Now put the siren on and let's get out of this line." Mr. King opened the top and put the siren on. On top of the car, the sound became loud and to be honest it sounded real. He turned the wheel to escape the line and started speeding. On the way, we got some people opening their windows, yelling, and cursing at us. Maybe they picked up on the police act since our car didn't really look like one.

"Okay, this is the plan. I have a gun in the back of the car. I'm licensed to carry it so it's not illegal; you go in and be careful. Have me on speed dial and call me if you find anything. Kayla will come with me." As we entered the space to the building, Mr. King dropped me off. I waved to both of them and stood in front of the building.

It was a big brown square with rusty doors. There was graffiti on the walls that had pictures of cartoons and people's names on it. There was an old smell that came through the shattered door. I walked through the broken glass and kicked open what was left of the door. A black hallway was in front of me and I didn't know which way to go, so I chose the one on my right. There were other doors in the walls. It looked like this was an old school or training room for gymnastics because there was a bar and mats in the rooms I passed by. I kept walking forward and saw a door open by itself. I walked to the door and went inside the room.

The room was completely empty. I saw broken mirrors and there in the middle of the floor in front of me I saw the box.

Chapter 25

I ran to the box and kneeled on the floor. I pulled out my phone and called Mr. King.

"What is it, Kody?" he asked.

"I found the box. It's weird though."

"Why is it weird?" he asked.

"Because it's just here with no one around."

"I'll be right in with the key." I hung up the phone and touched the box. I tried to understand why it was here. I picked it up and moved it around, then placed it back on the floor.

A few minutes later, after waiting for Mr. King who still hadn't shown up, I saw a body in the dark light. "Who is it?" I shouted. I tried to find a light switch, but only half of the room was bright because of the windows. Maybe this was it for me. No one could hear me scream or cry.

The body was muscular, but not fat. The hands were folded into a ball and the person's hair was short and brushed to the side. I looked back to the door and could hear footsteps running and I knew it was Kayla and Mr. King.

I turned in the other direction where the person was and the figure was gone. It was like nothing was there. God, it was like I was losing my mind. I was sure, though, that I saw it. Mr. King came running in with a gun in his side pocket. Kayla was behind him holding the eye necklace.

"What is it?" Mr. King asked.

"I saw someone in the shadow. It looked like a boy." Then I heard a voice." Hello."

I turned around and it was Carter crossing his arms.

"What are you doing here?" I asked him as I walked closer.

"I see you got the necklace unglued." He laughed a little.

"Carter, this isn't funny."

"It's completely."

"What is wrong with you? You're not yourself."

Then from the right came another person. "Of course he is," someone said in a female voice. It was the principal of our school.

"Why are you here?" said Mr. King.

"What do you think?" The principal's words left her mouth that was stained with a red lipstick.

I looked at Mr. King and he was just staring at her and then an expression hit his face that I couldn't explain.

"It was you." What was he talking about? "You are the one that killed Ronnie! You were the one who was after him!" The principal put her hand on Carter's shoulder and they looked at each other.

"Well, actually, I didn't kill him exactly."

"Then who did?" Kayla sobbed.

Another person emerged from the darkness behind them. He was taller and leaner. There weren't any more characteristics that I could recognize. The person came out into the light and my eyes dropped out of my face. It was like the earth was drowning me under its several oceans. It was my father.

Chapter 26

"You killed Kayla's father? " I asked. I was too shocked to ask anything more.

"Don't look so sad, it wasn't that bad, he didn't cry, much."

Kayla didn't say anything. She just kept looking at my father.

"Does my mom know you're here?" I asked.

"No, and you're not going tell her," he said, coming to me. I ran to grab the box.

"Mr. King." I threw it to him and Kayla opened the box.

"Get it, Carter!" the principal said, pushing him.

"Carter, stay away from Kayla and Mr. King," I said.

"Like you can beat me? I got powers too," he said. Was that what the scars were from?

I turned to my dad. "The bullet. You did this too, you were the one who crashed our car and shot Carter.

"Well, I shot Carter but the principal stole the car and hit you," my father responded.

"Kody, you gotta come here," Kayla said.

"Carter, get the stone!" the principal said. Suddenly, a dusty flash hit Kayla and she wiped out. I ran to her. "Kayla! What did you do to her?" I shouted to Carter.

"Well, my power is draining people's energy."

"But you haven't met mine." I placed my hand on Kayla's heart and I let my power heal her. I knew she wouldn't wake now, but she was breathing again.

I stood up and took the stone from the box. I started to walk toward them. "Why have you been after me? Why do you want me?" I asked.

"We want to figure out how this all started so we can create more of you."

"Can't you just accept he is the only one in the world who has this?" said Mr. King. "All the testing to do what you want can kill him."

"But it's worth it," the principal said. She took out something from her pocket that looked like a bottle of potion.

She stepped forward in front of Carter. "Give it to me."

"What will the stone do?"

"It will take away your powers which will be placed in the stone," Mr. King said.

"And you knew this the whole time?" I said.

"I had to be sure before I told you," Mr. King said, backing up my accusation that was obviously true.

"I said give it!"

"No," my voice again becoming demonic.

I threw the stone to Mr. King. Simultaneously, Carter and I placed our hands in front and battled each other with our flash powers. I pushed so hard, but I could feel Carter pushing harder. I looked to the principal and saw her give the potion to my dad. He opened the bottle cap and poured it onto Carter's flash. The look on Carter's face was evil; like he had won. The fact that my father would do anything like this, was too horrid to imagine. The liquid mixed and shot out with Carter's flash.

I had no idea what was coming for me, besides the paralyzing pain. It hit me and I was out. I had a glimpse of Kayla and Mr. King running to me and I knew it wasn't good. The light blinded me and I had no choice but to give up. Those were the murderous words that sent me over the edge. "Give up." But right now, I knew I had nothing left. I saw the flash, then blackness, but it was more than that, it was..... a nightmare.

CPSIA information can be obtained
at www.ICGtesting.com
Printed in the USA
BVHW03s0041270818
525684BV00001B/12/P